HERE BE DRAGONS

Janae V. Seldura

ISBN 9798590603442

Printed in the United States
of America. Book Design by Janae
Vasquez Seldura

CONTENTS

I like a man who grins when he fights.
-Winston Churchill

HERE BE DRAGONS

<u>Chapter 1: The Blitz Warden</u>

There once was a time when London was ravaged by dragons. These dragons were ruthless and mighty creatures; like others of their kind, they roared, and flew, and spat fire upon whatever unfortunate city they sought to plunder. Now, these particular creatures convened during the cool of the day so they could strike all through the night. And once they had their fill of destruction and ichor, they would fly off and bellow with triumph and mockery until they returned. They did not spare any town or city; the rich, the poor, the large, and the small were all raided by these monstrous beasts. And it did not take them long to set their scorching gaze towards the heart of England itself.

Of course, the Londoners tried their best to evade the fiery wrath of these monsters. The year was 1940, and the British decided that for now, their sharpest weapons were knowledge and discernment. Everyone knows that if you cannot defeat a dragon, you can hide from it. Thus, a plethora of odd and specific rules had been established by the country's governing heads.

"Stay inside, stay inside!" They urged. "Do stock up on food and essentials. Never vacate your dwelling at night. If you turn on your lamp, close your curtain! The beasts are attracted to light!"

Because of the charm of the jingle and the immense fear of being burnt to a crisp, the people quickly obeyed; every night at exactly 8 o'clock, London became wholly gloomier than ever before. Without the shine of the streetlamps or the glow from neighbouring windows, the entire city remained dark, and dead, and dull until morning.

London also lacked young, healthy lads at the time. Most of them, aged eighteen to forty-one, were sent overseas to slay the dragons with guns and daggers and other swift weapons. But no matter how hard the governing heads tried to tear their citizens from their families and ship them away to go fight, the beasts still threatened to shed blood.

Now, the evening the dragons came seemed just like any other. It was quiet and black and lifeless outside, and most of the city had already gone to bed and shut off their lights. But some people in the tall flat right above the local spectacle shop near River Thames were still awake and about. On the middle floor lived a family of three, which included a middle-aged wife and a middle-aged husband and their very young niece. But right above, at the very tippy-top floor, lived a glassmaker.

London still had many of them. Like the butchers and bakers and candlestick makers, they were considered too important to go dragon-slaying. Whether it be for the chalices at the pub or for the coloured windows at the Church, glass was far too valuable for the English to forsake. So indeed, all those who worked for Ye Olde Glass Shoppes were spared from the fires of war; every single day of the week, they resumed work as normal and created whatever glass products the city required.

But this is a story about the glassmaker who went to slay a dragon anyway.

He was a young man at the age of twenty-two. He had rather average-looking hair and an average-looking face. He wore average clothes and spoke in an average manner. But most of all, he had a rather average daily routine to go with it. Now that his work was done, he had already strolled home, washed up, and put on his white collared shirt and soft blue jumper with a stitched diamond pattern at the front. In his orderly, well-lit bedroom he remained, sitting comfortably at his polished, oak desk.

This particular glassmaker, who went by the name Thomas Atkins, was very busy inspecting a glass ship he had made the day before. It was blue and clear and about half a metre long. It was simple and round and cold to the touch. And it was made for a rather special purpose; it was not a commissioned piece of work he made with a certain amount of time and a certain amount of money. Instead, it was a gift he handcrafted for a dear friend who had gone overseas to slay the dragons.

Of course, you should never try to make a ship out of glass. For a small mischievous child might find it and snatch it and poke at it and toy with it and test if it floats in water. And that's exactly what happened next.

At the next moment, there was a knock at the door. Thomas knew who it was and tried to ignore it. He shut off his light, pretending to be fast asleep. But once the knock persisted and quickened and grew strong enough to shake the fragile square frames on the walls, he scoffed and sighed and opened the door.

On the mat right in front of him stood a child. She was small and freckled with her hands behind her back and her legs in a crisscrossed stance. She looked up with big, hazel eyes and gave a warm smile.

Thomas rolled his eyes in response.

It was none other than his young cousin, Millie May. She had lived with his parents in the middle floor for about three months now; her own mum and dad, who lived all the way in Cheshire, were quite busy having heated arguments about commitment and love and bills and inheritance and other bleak, ghastly things you might not wish to hear about. So, as a result, Mr. and Mrs. Atkins believed that it was best for their young niece to stay in London where it was safe.

But Thomas did not like Millie May. He pointed out the door and stomped his foot lightly.

"Oh no," said he, "you should go back to bed. Please get out. Out, out, out!"

With his arms crossed, he blocked the entrance and waited.

Of course, Millie May did not go out. Instead, she scurried right past her cousin and sat at his desk. With a small, dainty finger, she turned on the lights and pointed to the glass ship on the table.

"It's very pretty." she chirped, poking it until it wobbled. "Does it float? Does it? Does it?"

"Why, yes." Thomas groaned. "It does float. But not well. In rippling waters, it topples right over."

Before his cousin could grab ahold of the ship, he snatched it and placed it on a rather tall shelf.

"I value your words," he sighed, "but I see right through them. Just tell me. What is it that you want? Milk? Money? A pen?"

Millie May shook her head.

"No, I don't want any of that!" said she. "I need a favour instead."

"But I just offered you favours!"

"No, not that kind of favour! The other kind!"

The two glared at one another with annoyance. After a tense moment, Millie May sighed and spoke softly.

"Do you remember the soft red paper that your mum gave me? For my birthday?"

Pushing her big hair aside, she looked to the ground as Thomas nodded.

"Well," she continued, "the last piece I folded into an aeroplane. And...I threw it because I wanted to see if it could fly, but it went out of the window and into the street."

Before she could say any more, Thomas held up a finger.

"I know what you're thinking," he warned. "We can't go out until morning. You'll have to get it tomorrow. Do you want to trip and fall?"

But Millie May came prepared. She smirked and giggled and blinked teasingly. Out of her pocket, she withdrew a silver spoon and a small, colourful box. Then, she opened it and held it up in front of her cousin.

Inside, Thomas saw a pale, creamy substance. A pleasant, sugary smell ascended right from it. As it shined like diamonds in the lamplight, he felt his mouth water. Before he could lean over and take a closer look, Millie May closed the box shut.

"I'll give you all of this vanilla pudding and more," she proposed, "if you help me get my aeroplane. Please! I saw where it landed. Come with me to fetch it! I don't wish to go alone!"

Now, in any other circumstance, Thomas would have repeated the rules and urged his cousin out of the room. But in this situation, he complied in a heartbeat; quite far above books and baubles and money and gold, he valued and savoured the sweet taste of pudding.

"Very well," said he, "but we must be back soon! 'Tis a fool's sport to run in the dark."

Down the winding stairs they went. They dared not turn on any lights, for fear that the Air Raid Police would knock at the door. Luckily, Thomas knew his father's spectacle shop inside and out; holding his cousin's hand, he dashed around every desk and drawer and table and chair.

Once they unlocked the front door and hopped out onto the stone path, they were consumed by the dark. All the street lamps and car lights were turned off and well hidden from view. Even the stars, shrouded in the thick clouds above, could not offer their light.

The two stood on the cold stone pavement without making a sound. After some waiting, Thomas turned to his cousin.

"Well?" he asked uneasily. "Well, where is it?"

Millie May looked around and said nothing. With her left hand, she reached into her pocket once more and grabbed a smooth, silver object. After fumbling around with it, she held it up high and pressed her finger on something inside. There was a sharp *click* and a *whoosh*, and out of nowhere, in the middle of the box, danced a tiny flame.

Thomas inhaled sharply and gasped in horror.

"Where did you get- have you been smoking?" he cried. He tried to grab the lighter from her hand but she pulled away swiftly.

"No," his cousin replied, "I traded it."

"You traded it? With whom?"

"Well, that part matters not! But now it is mine. And that matters so!"

Giggling, she sprinted forward, letting the flame from the pipe lighter direct her path. She held it in front of the fence and the walls and the plants and the stones, watching her tall shadow bounce and stretch as she ran.

Thomas, of course, was not as amused. He strolled uncomfortably, scouring the area for anyone who might see them. The orange light was horribly indiscreet; though it came from the smallest wisp of fire, it shone so brightly that the next three neighbouring flats could be seen. Before a full minute had passed, Thomas put his foot down.

"Millie May, shut off that light!" he fussed. "This has gone far enough! You've had your fun. Now either hurry up or hurry away!"

Of course, his cousin did not shut off the light. She galloped towards the edge of the gate and held the lighter well above her head.

"There it is!" she squealed, pointing to the block of flats right across the street. Upon its wooden door stood a flagpole that donned a noble, waving Union Jack. Pierced through it, thin as it was, sat the wing of the poor scarlet plane. Like a waning, skewered animal, it fluttered for a while in the wind and stood still.

Thomas sprinted towards the gate. He took a quick gander at the plane on the end of the flagpole and shook his head.

"Oh, pity," he sighed, "the finial has stabbed right through it. I don't suppose it can fly again. Come, now. Let us go back."

But Millie May only laughed.

"Oh, I knew that," she mused, "I told you that I saw where it landed. I just wanted to go outside! And here we are."

In response, Thomas put his hands on his hips.

"Well, that's just lovely," he muttered, "but that pudding belongs to me. And we're going to go home right this instant. Come on!"

He reached out to grab his cousin's hand. But before he could do so, a rather large shadow swiftly passed over them.

Thomas blinked and narrowed his eyes. He swore the shadow had two wings and a tail. Looking around and behind him, he sighed in relief and figured that it came from his imagination.

The cold winds howled ominously. Another winged shadow passed by. It was larger and darker and it shook the ground in its wake. As it departed, a strong breeze rushed forward and extinguished the lighter's tiny flame. Confused and quite alarmed, the two shivered and shook in the sudden darkness.

"Millie May," Thomas whispered, "do you hear me?"

His cousin held his hand tighter.

"Yes," she replied, "I do. Quite well, actually."

"Good. Now stay close behind. And follow the sound of my voice."

Thomas paused and took a step. But just as he set his foot down, he heard a thundering crash.

A flash of hot light and smoke followed. It blew the top stone chunks of the surrounding buildings to bits. Thomas let go of his cousin's hand and covered his face with his arms. Blinded and deafened by clouds of brown debris, he stumbled and waved at the thick air around him.

He could barely hear his own breathing. Before he could call out for help, another flaming blast struck the side of the spectacle shop and sent him flying onto the stone road. He tumbled to the ground. His head hit something hard. For a second, he saw billowing smog and wavering flames creep upward. Dazed by the impact, he closed his eyes and lay still.

When he awoke, his head throbbed and pounded. He hadn't moved from his spot at all. Coughing and spitting, he rubbed his stinging eyes and groaned. The ground beneath him was shaking. Beside him, the lawn was set ablaze. Thomas grasped his sooty head, got up on his feet, and spun around.

"Hullo?" he cried out. "Mum? Dad? Millie May? Anyone!"

He heard crackling and popping and some harsh, smashing noises. With a sharp ringing in his ears, he looked upon his house and gaped at what he saw.

A large, cavernous hole ripped through the roof. It hardly resembled a building at all. Its skeleton, composed of a steel frame with layered stone, was jagged and torn and exposed to the world. Thomas bit his lip as he watched his home burn. Before he could step forward, he heard a loud whistle.

Running down the street behind him was a rather stout man. His long, blue coat trailed behind him as he sprinted. He wore a beige gas mask and a dark blue steel helmet with a white letter 'W' painted on its front.

Resisting the urge to cry, Thomas bolted towards the man and opened the gate.

"Ho, Constable!" he yelled, gasping for breath. "The house! The street! We, they all, just- why, have you seen-"

"Oh, hush now," snapped the warden, "do you have a shelter on your property?"

Thomas froze. He had to think for a second or two.

"We do!" he finally sputtered. "We have- here, near the gate. Are they-"

"Well? Alrighty, then. Do get inside it."

"W-wait! We can find them. I'll even help you. Please, don't-"

"Shut it! Get inside or else. No use being out here in the explosions unprotected, lad. Now go!"

Thomas frowned. He looked around worriedly and panted as the smoky air rang with screams and wails. As the noises grew louder, he was filled with deep dread.

"No!" he yelled.

As he tried to turn around and run back towards the burning building, the warden grabbed his shoulders. Trying to break free, Thomas yelped and grabbed him back in response.

Before long, a scuffle broke out. In the heat of the explosions, they grappled and fought, seizing each other's limbs whilst yelling and grunting like madmen.

Eventually, poor Thomas, who was unable to overpower his opponent, was seized by the neck and pushed back. Before he could swing his arm forward, the warden struck him in the forehead and all turned dark.

Chapter 2: Edwin's Dilemma

Up in the middle floor, things weren't much better. Before the bombs struck, Mr. and Mrs. Atkins were sipping tea in their room, talking about boring grownup things that somehow kept them awake.

But when the fires came and shot the side of their building, the two dropped their glass china and froze. Mr. Edwin, who was usually a slow and sluggish gentleman, grasped his wife's hand with tight speed.

"Emelia," he barked, "get under the table!" He covered his face with his forearm as the wall was blown to bits and the side of the flat crumbled down. Emelia jumped and looked around in great distress. Before she could duck and cover, she halted.

"Edwin, wait!" said she, "the children!"

Sprinting over shattered glass, she broke free from her husband's grasp and searched her niece's room. Upon realising that Millie May was gone, she ran off, kicked down the burning door, and raced up towards Thomas's dwelling. Before she could grab her spare key and twist the doorknob open, another blast came and knocked her to the ground.

Of course, Edwin could have saved her if he knew this had happened. But at this time, he was still taking cover with his hands and knees on the wooden floor. As the blasts grew louder, he tried his best to crawl away. Before he could go scurry off elsewhere, he halted, for the floor was riddled with loud embers, glass shards, and broken metal pipes.

Dazed and quite helpless, he flinched as the ground shook. But out of the rumbling and the tumbling and through the hissing steam came bold, barking voices. At the side of the flat, through the wide, gaping hole in the building, hopped a small squad of masked wardens. They jumped from a thin, tall ladder and searched with their torches and sharp, prodding sticks. One of them flipped the table over, grabbed Edwin by the hand, and helped him down onto the street.

"Do wait," Edwin choked, waving the smoke away from his face. "What of the others? My wife, she-"

"Oh, we'll find them, we will," said one of the officers, "but get to your shelter, and we'll take it from here."

Poor Edwin had no choice but to listen. He staggered towards the door on the lawn and took refuge, shakily waiting and hoping for his kin to join him. After a few long minutes, his wishes were granted true. Soon, the warden chief came and knocked thrice at the hatch. As the orange sky darkened and roared, he dropped Edwin's unconscious son at the front and ran off.

Thomas woke up in a cold and dusty room. The metal walls all around vibrated and shook and rattled every few seconds. Underneath him was a hard, cushioned mattress with a thin, scratchy blanket draped across. Right at his sides stood wooden shelves stocked with cans and sandbags and cases of water.

At first, he thought he was brought to a hospital.

"Is anyone there?" he called out, grasping the sheets and coughing a bit.

Nobody answered. He sat up and put a hand to his head. Under his aching, calloused fingers, he felt a soft bandage wrapped snugly around it. By his side flickered a lantern that was fastened against the wall. Before he could inspect it some more, he saw someone enter the room.

The man was none other than Edwin Atkins. His dark suit was blackened and torn. On his face, he had a pair of cracked spectacles and half of a bristled, sandy-blonde moustache. He looked at Thomas with saddened eyes.

"Dad?" Thomas choked. He tried to swing his legs over the bed and onto the dirt ground, but they ached quite horrendously.

"Be still," said Edwin, placing a gentle hand on Thomas's shoulder. With his other, he silently lit a match to fuel the lantern.

Thomas watched in silence.

"The shelter...we're in the shelter!" he croaked. He coughed a few times and wiped his moist face. Edwin nodded. He dropped the dead match in his pocket and rubbed the dust off of his hand.

"Why, Mum and Millie May," Thomas whispered, "are they here too?"

He wheezed and shivered a little as Edwin grimaced, sighed, and shook his large head.

"No," he answered, "the wardens said they would look for them. Why, I...haven't heard anything since."

Brushing his dirty hair, he sat on the bed and stared at the wall. Thomas flinched and looked away. A wave of guilt seeped into his gut. In his head, he imagined a plethora of possible scenarios. Finally, he burst into tears.

"This is all my fault," he sobbed, refusing to make eye contact. "'Twas me! I did it. I went outside with Millie May to fetch her aeroplane. Why, if I had been more stern with her, then she would have stayed and sought refuge with you. Mum would have never gone up to fetch us. And now, both of them might be dead and gone!"

He covered his ashen face in shame. Closing his eyes and pressing a fist to his forehead, he tried to recall what had happened right before he was brought down to safety.

He remembered something about the Air Raid Police but could not put the pieces together. In frustration, he leapt from the bed, left the room, and limped to the shelter's door. To his father's dismay, he clicked the latch and swung the hatch open.

Outside, as expected, in the midst of the fires and the explosions, ran dozens and dozens of wardens. It appeared that they were brave, noble folk; with their gas masks and helmets and sharp, blue suits, they ran all over the streets and did what they could. While some worked to extinguish the fires with waterlogged hosepipes, others carried unconscious citizens over their shoulders and onto long stretchers. As they dodged flying debris and helped people out of their homes, they chanted a strong, rhythmic song that sounded something like this:

Quench with water, quench with sand!
Heave, ho! Carry and throw!
Steady arm and steady hand
And tell that beast to go!

One in particular was not singing or helping. Instead, he stood right in the middle of the street with his hands behind his back. As the others ran around saving men and women and children and pets, he oversaw the action and barked angry orders.

Thomas swore he had seen the man before. He did not like this one bit. As he slowly remembered what had occurred, he popped his head out of the lowly door and shouted.

"Oi, you!" he yelled. "Yes, you. Don't act like you don't recall. You were the one who threw me in here, hm? Care to explain yourself?"

The warden, however, did not say a word. Quick as lightning, he reached to his side and pulled out a small, silver handgun. With horrifying speed, he whirled around and pulled the trigger. Thomas let out a cry as a loud bullet ricocheted off of the ground near his head. It missed by nearly a centimetre. Not knowing what to say, he stared at his attacker in terror.

Never before had someone tried to shoot him. In all his years, he had only witnessed a few short fights in the glass shop and on the streets near the pubs. He had seen films and shows and plays that featured fake guns and their awful effects. But never ever, in all his life, had he been shot at.

He whimpered and fled and shut the door with great haste. Edwin soon rushed over and grabbed him as he slinked down onto the cold floor below.

"It's no use," Thomas choked. "We're stuck down here! But we need to get answers. We need to go-"

Right before he could say another word, a heavy explosion from above shook the ground. The shelter and its contents wobbled a bit, driving Thomas and his father against the wall. In the midst of the chaos, Edwin ran towards the lantern and grabbed it just in time.

"I'm afraid we'll just have to wait," said he, "for them to send us a letter. We have no telephone in here; I was a fool to leave that bit out. Until we are informed of the whereabouts of your mother and cousin, I'm afraid we'll have to avoid dwelling on it, hm?"

And with that, the two looked at one another and sighed.

They drank cold tea that night. For days and days, they waited and waited. With naught but a pocket watch and a jotter, the two created a chart that recorded their mealtimes and rations. When there was not much to clean or fix or prepare, they sat around on their beds or paced back and forth with their hands behind their backs and their heads down low.

Sometimes, when the inside became way too hot, they would pop open the hatch and seek fresher air. Unfortunately, it was not much better above-ground; as the bombs continued to drop, the smoke had thickened while the harsh winds reeked of charcoal, sulfur, and blood. To make matters worse, the warden chief still patrolled the streets with his gun in his hand. Every time he came close, Thomas and his father had to duck and hide before he could spot them.

Getting sufficient sleep was another concern. Every few minutes or so, the two would hear a new, ghastly noise such as a boom or a scream or something they could not describe in words. Each night, they shivered in their beds and wondered if the shelter was going to collapse on itself any second. With every tremor and judder and quiver and quake, the metal walls creaked as the loose, dry dirt trickled down from the ceiling.

Minutes felt like hours. Hours felt like days. Days felt like years. Nearly a week had passed by and for the most part, each moment felt exactly as the one before. As the sun rose and fell above the smog, all that went on in between was marked by orderly chaos and unforeseen constant.

To make matters worse, they heard no news of Emelia or Millie May. Their absence crossed their minds more often than not, but they wished not to speak about it at all. One day, Thomas noticed that his father was especially quiet. For hours on end, he stared at the lantern and watched it pulse in the dark. Thomas tilted his head and shifted uncomfortably. After struggling to put together a question, he whimpered, coughed, and spoke up.

"You've been staring at that light as if it were a film," said he. "If I must ask, what are you thinking?"

It took a long while for Edwin to notice. With glassy eyes, he blinked fast and looked at his son.

"I'm sorry. What did you say?" he muttered, scratching his chin.

"I asked what you are thinking. You're as still as a stone, you are. Are you alright? Is there much I can do?"

Edwin nodded and laughed quite glumly. He scratched his scalp and sat up straight.

"Nothing," he answered. "Nothing at all."

Of course, Thomas knew that there was certainly something. He valued good words but always saw through them. After this, the two did not say much for the rest of the night.

The next day, Edwin did not wish to get up from his bed. For a long while, he lay on his side, staring at the wall and remaining silent. At first, Thomas thought he was sick. He placed a hand on his father's back and offered him a bowl of soup on a tray. After a good moment, Edwin spoke up.

"Away," he croaked. "Why, they'll send you away."

Thomas blinked in confusion. He cocked his head and wondered for a while.

"Away?" he asked, putting the tray on the ground. "What...do you mean by that?"

"For too long," said Edwin, "you have dodged the draft, with your occupation and all. But now that you're stuck down here with me, they'll take you away. They'll send you off to go fight, they will."

Thomas blinked once more. He grumbled quickly and shook his head.

"Dad, you're not thinking straight," he responded. "England will always need glass as long as the shops are still open. And if not, I'll find another job, I will. Now you get some rest. You need it so!"

"Oh, so you'll find one?" Edwin growled. He shot up from his position and glared at his son. "And when will that be? Have you looked? What exactly have you done these last few days?"

Thomas shuddered. He felt his knees wobble.

"I'm s-sorry?" he huffed, "Dad, I can't just leave. It's not safe! I'm afraid there's not much that I- I mean...we can d-do...This isn't anyone's fault!"

"Not anyone's fault? Was fighting the warden a good idea? Or breaking the rules and taking your cousin outside? Your mum left to find the two of you, and now she's gone. You said it yourself. This is quite your fault, this is!"

"W-well, it all happened so fast! My goodness, Dad," Thomas cried. "Where is this coming from?"

But Edwin was not listening. He continued to grumble and scream and berate his son. In a fit of rage, he grasped their unlit lantern and threw it upon the ground. With a terrible noise, it smashed and burst into pieces.

They did not speak at all since. Thomas did not get any sleep that night, either, for he was far too disturbed by what he had heard. Lying on his side, he choked and tried to hold back hot tears. Finally, on the seventh day of this fiendish quarantine, he could take it no longer. At around three in the morning, whilst his father slept, he had planned a means of escape. With a near-dry pen and a crumpled piece of parchment, he wrote a quick letter that went as follows:

Dad,

> *I am terribly sorry, but if you are reading this note, I have gone off to look for Mum and Millie May. When I return, I will have their location, along with some more rations and linens and anything else that we are lacking. 'Tis true that you and I cannot stand this ill treatment much longer. Thus, if you awaken and find that I am missing from my bedding, it means that I have gone to look for answers and ways to improve our current predicament.*

> *If I do not return by midday, please do not assume the worst; it is likely that the roads are quite blocked or I am presently waiting for the authorities to check their records. Once again, I apologise if this decision seems rash or foolhardy; I will try my best to stay safe. Farewell!*

Sincerely,

Thomas

Placing the letter on his bed, he grabbed a spare gas mask and tiptoed to the hatch. Swinging it open, he watched carefully for any wardens lurking about. Once the coast was clear and the air was still, he crawled onto the stone road and stayed low to the ground.

His shoulders spiked up in fear. With sweat on his brow, he kept looking behind him to see if his father would pop out the door and urge him to come back. In his head, he felt like he was being watched. But still, no one came. After a bit of trudging and groaning, he approached the front gate. It towered over him and cast a strong shadow. He rubbed his hands and shuddered. But before he could pry it open, he heard the piercing sound of a gunshot.

Thomas covered his head. His breathing quickened. Slowly, he looked up and saw someone hop right out of a wrecked building.

It was none other than the warden chief, holding his silver gun. The glass goggles on his mask shone bright, like two glowing eyes. In front of him jogged three more officers, scanning the area as well. Thomas froze. His thoughts raced around in all kinds of directions, unable to decide if he should duck or hide or run or stay still.

The chief looked around for a bit and inspected the floor. He turned his head around slowly, eyeing the gate. But right before he could look below it, a rather marvelous thing had happened. With an ear-splitting smash, the great stone building to his right collapsed over him.

In response, the wardens around the area fled. Screaming and shouting, they dodged shards of hot metal and billowing smoulders.

Thomas flinched. Once the streets were clear, he took a few shallow breaths and seized his chance. He huffed and puffed and charged towards the gate, swinging it open. As he sprinted onto the road, he passed by the crumbled building where the chief had once stood. He stopped and stared at the rubble, looking for the dead body. But as he squinted at the scene, he took notice of something. There, in between a large cobblestone split in two, sat the blue scratched helmet. Its chipped edge gleamed with light from the fires.

Thomas cupped his hand under his chin. He had an idea. Pushing the stones aside, he snatched the helmet by the rim and placed it on his head. Looking down, however, he gasped at a rather grisly sight.

Though the warden's mask was still intact, one of the glass lenses had shattered, revealing a widened, terrified, crystal-blue eye.

Thomas gagged, closed his eyes, and took a reluctant step forward. He sheepishly grabbed the chief's limp arm, pulling the dead man away from the rocks. After some grunting and straining, he removed the navy blue uniform and clothed himself in it.

He scoffed. It was too large; the scratchy sleeves dangled past his fingers and the coat trailed down to his thighs. Whilst carefully looking around for witnesses, he folded and tucked the extra fabric in his belt and scurried towards the heart of the town itself.

Into the burning city he ran. He searched around for the Air Raid Police, biting his lip and hoping that the disguise looked convincing. While his mask had filled up with steam, it shielded him from the filthy, black air that so plagued the atmosphere. Though its rubber skin and tight straps made the surrounding noises sound muffled, the vibrating road and rising smoke gave him stark warnings of where new explosions had hit.

Up above, shiny flocks of metal beasts dashed across the skies. Thomas dared not look up. With his eyes fixed ahead, he dashed clumsily around broken cars, pulverised houses, and shattered glass. Once he had reached the town square, he cowered behind a heap of steel beams.

Ahead, in the fires, more officers ran amuck. They swarmed in and out of surrounding shops, moving harmful, flammable materials and clearing a path on the road. Two of them were carrying an older fellow on a stretcher, ducking and shouting and watching their step.

Thomas squinted and watched for a minute. He wondered if the poor man they found was dead, unconscious, or simply asleep. Regardless, he figured that the wardens had answers. After some brief thinking, he decided to follow them and learn where they were headed.

He pursued them through alleyways and corridors and under torn bridges. Through broken buses and burning signs they hurried, avoiding open patches of land. Finally, at the end of a rather long street, the wardens halted. They nodded and looked to their left and their right. As they tiptoed to a cracked sidewalk tile, the one at the rear withdrew a small bell and rang it twice.

Thomas watched as a third masked officer ascended from a flight of stairs that led underground. With great haste he turned on a torch, made way for the others, and scurried down behind them. Thomas bit his lip, panted, and dashed towards the stairs. With a *click-clack* and a *tip-tap,* he hobbled down the steps until it was too dark to see.

<u>Chapter 3: Eyes of Glass</u>

The stairwell was eerie, frigid, and damp. The *drip-drip* of the black dewdrops echoed and resounded through the great, descending hall of old steps. Thomas pressed on and on for what seemed like hours. Part of his mind was convinced this was all a bad dream. Unable to catch up to the others, he lost sight of the rear warden's torchlight and held onto the rail in fear. Just when he was about to stop and take a rest, he saw a small, flickering light down below.

He removed his mask to get a better look. Indeed, right at the very bottom, shone a miniscule yellow dot. Shrouded by mist, it glimmered stubbornly like a lone star. Thomas beamed and rushed down the stairwell. Slipping a few times but still gaining speed, he hurried down, down, down, until he reached the very bottom.

He galloped onto a glossy tile floor. The room he had entered was dark, and chilly, and spacious, and wide; its brick ceiling stretched high above, curving in an arc that trembled slightly. Around it hung flickering, dying lights that popped, fizzed, and swung to and fro.

Ahead was a tunnel. Far off into the dark it continued, stretching down endlessly like the throat of a giant beast. Below it sat a railroad track covered in blankets and trinkets and rags and bags. And in between these muddled piles of items sat dozens and dozens of masked Londoners, muttering and sleeping and shaking and coughing.

Thomas marveled at the sight. He tried to recall the last time he had seen so many people huddled together at once. He stood awkwardly and looked to his left. The wavering light he had seen on the stairwell turned out to be a very small flame. It continued to shine, overpowering whatever brightness the ceiling lamps failed to deliver. He watched as it danced over a metal pipe lighter, which was held by a frail, hunchbacked figure. It brought the lighter to its face, revealing the pale, charred gas mask it wore on its head.

"Over," the man rasped, coughing as he spoke.

"I...beg your pardon?" Thomas replied. He cocked his head as the man respired noisily.

"When will it be over? The beasts. Are they gone?"

Thomas opened his mouth to respond. But before he could utter a word, dozens of glass eyes stared right at him. Taking a step back, he squeaked and shivered as more masked Londoners crept out of the shadows and climbed onto the platform.

"The beasts!" they cried, "Are they gone? Do tell us!"

They shouted and wailed, sobbing and begging for information and answers. Thomas put on his mask and tried to run. As he pushed through the crowd, they pushed back even harder. Before long, a swarm of desperate hands grabbed at his shoulders, arms, and hair.

"Oh, how I am finished!" Thomas cried. He knew not what else to do or say. But just as he was about to slink back and give up, he was saved.

"You let him go!" barked a slew of commanding voices. The assailants froze and looked in the direction from whence it came.

Indeed, the noise came from an onslaught of angry wardens, who shoved the citizens aside and dragged Thomas out of the mess. As the crowd fought back, two guards escorted the poor man down the tunnel and into the dark to safety. Though relieved, Thomas shook in his uneven uniform.

Good God, it ends here! he thought. *Perhaps they have seen through my disguise. Oh, how I am helpless!*

He started to regret leaving the shelter and grabbing the coat and running through the streets. Inhaling sharply, he quivered at the thought of going to prison for impersonating an officer or worse. He closed his eyes as he walked. But once they all hurried to an old ticket booth, the wardens began to speak softly and kindly.

"I'm afraid they've been getting more restless, Chief." muttered one.

"Yes, indeed," said the other, "and it's only been a week. These poor souls could be here for months on end, by the looks of it. So, do tell us! What are your orders?"

Thomas stuttered. He cleared his throat and looked down awkwardly.

"W-well," he muttered, trying his best to make his voice deep and gruff, "I suppose you should keep doing what you were doing before. Why, I came down to check if a...certain family was brought here to the underground. Who among you might provide a keen answer, hm? Who?"

The wardens thought and nodded and put their hands at their backs.

"Why, the nurses, of course!" they answered in unison. "They've got every record and every name written in their heads and on parchment. Come, let us go to the infirmary! Anything for you, dear sir."

And with that, the three went off to find the nurses. They sprinted up and down stairs and through secret halls. No matter where they wandered and went, they were barricaded and questioned by throngs of masked people. Some lay down in great piles while others strung hammocks between the platforms and tracks. All around sat dark heaps of coats, boxes, umbrellas, and hats.

The air was not clean. It reeked with a hopeless aura. Thomas shuddered as he observed his surroundings. He tried to imagine how many citizens were rescued and brought to the underground the day the dragons came. In his head, he counted all the neighbours and acquaintances he had spoken to in the past and wondered how many were alive and how many were dead. It bothered him much. Shivering at these ghastly thoughts, he shook his head and kept going.

At the end of the tunnel, where an old, lone passenger coach remained in its spot, was an improvised infirmary. Thomas knew this when he saw the cots on the ground. Sprawled on these dirtied white sheets were patients of all ages, staring at the lights above or sleeping through the noises. Some had bandages on their heads and hands while others were getting their eyes and ears checked. Those who were coughing and sneezing were placed far, far away from the rest.

Thomas and the others soon found the nurses, who, with their bloodied skirts and worn-down shoes, walked in and out of the coach quite hurriedly. Many of them donned rusted gas masks and unkempt hair. Some leaned against the walls to get a quick breather only to be called by a whimpering child or an incomer on a stretcher.

Thomas frowned and shuffled his feet. He felt quite sorry for the nurses. He took a step forward to get a closer look at what they were doing. But when one of them saw him enter the room, she nearly dropped what she was holding.

"Why, the chief is here!" she shrieked. "Places, everyone!"

In the blink of an eye, the area was tidied up quite well. The frantic nurses ran back and forth, sweeping the floors and picking up rubbish. Once they were done, they stood in a row and placed their frail arms at their sides.

Thomas bit his lip under his mask. He tried to think of what to say. After crafting a quick and clumsy lie, he rubbed his clammy hands together. Walking forward quite awkwardly, he pulled one of the nurses to the side and whispered in her ear.

"I have an enquiry about the census," said he, "yes, a warden lost count and I have an ill, faulty record. Pray tell me! Have you heard news of a lass named Emelia Atkins?"

The nurse thought for a bit. And then she spoke.

"Why, yes," she replied, "I remember the name. In fact, she's here, Chief."

Thomas gasped. He panted heavily, trying to contain his excitement and relief. Before he could lose his focus, he closed his eyes and maintained his composure.

"If that be the case," he continued, "then I would like to speak with her privately. I've got pressing questions for her, I do. Care to show me?"

The nurse nodded stiffly. She marched towards the coach and gestured for Thomas to follow. Around the large structure he went, ordering the others to carry about their business.

They found Emelia lying on a cot at the end of the rail. Facing the wall, she was in the corner all by herself and with her eyes shut. As promised, the nurse left the two alone. Thomas removed his helmet and placed it on the cold ground. The silver buttons on his large coat made a soft *clink* as he fell to his knees.

"Mum," he whispered, prodding her shoulder. "Mum, are you alright? It's me."

He stroked her hair and tapped her shoulder repeatedly. For a long moment, she did not wake. Thomas shook her gently and continued to call out to her. But before he could despair, she yawned and opened her right eye.

"E-Edwin?" she mumbled, turning her head slightly. "Edwin, is that you?"

Thomas gave a heavy sigh of relief and sniffled.

"No, no. No, it's not. It's me. It's me, Thomas. I came here, I- I came all the way here."

With tears in his eyes, he wrapped his arms around her head and took in her scent. After giving her a tight, prolonged hug, he inched back, expecting a response.

But Emelia did not say anything. She did not even look in his direction. Instead, her eyes shifted around slightly and stared at the tall ceiling above.

Thomas's smile faded. He sensed that something was wrong.

"Mum...are you alright? Why won't you look at me?"

He looked in her direction and waved while Emelia sighed.

"Well," said she, "I'm afraid I cannot."

Thomas cocked his head at her statement. He repeated it under his breath and narrowed his eyes. But when his mother sat up and looked in his direction, he knew.

With a balled fist, she rubbed at her left eye. It was filmy and glasslike. The other was covered by a sooty bandage wrapped around her head and hair. Her brown curls, once whole and thick and healthy, were damaged and slightly singed on the left side. No matter where she looked and how hard, she did not react or draw attention to anything at all.

Thomas felt his weary heart drop. He desperately waved a hand in front of her face. And yet, she did not respond.

"I- it's…" he choked. "You're-"

He lifted the bandage and winced at what he saw. Her left eye, and whatever else made up that side of her face, were marked by a streak of red, singed flesh.

Thomas gently lowered the gauze and looked down.

"Is there no cure?" he whimpered, choking on tears.

"I'm afraid not."

"Do you remember? What happened?"

"A little."

Thomas wailed. For the next few moments, they said nothing. Finally, Emelia closed her right eye and lay down.

"And what of my cousin?" Thomas cried. "Where is she?"

"Oh, it's awful!" Emelia choked. "They found her, but there was nothing more they could do. She was already gone when they arrived."

Soon, Thomas found himself staring into the darkness as well. He covered his nose and his mouth, trying to remember the last few things he said to his cousin. For quite a bit of time, he sobbed with his mother, trying to think of what else to do.

"But Dad," Thomas choked. "If only Dad knew. Why, he would die of great grief if he heard!"

He paused for a moment and looked to the floor.

"Dad...I'll have to tell him. M-maybe I can get him to move down here. I'll do it, I will. We'll all be together again, even if- even if y-you can't see..."

He hunched over and curled his fingers over his face. He winced as his joints felt numb and cold. Sniffling heavily, he wiped his tears away and cradled his mother in his arms.

They knew not how long they stayed together. Once Emelia felt the need to rest once more, Thomas got up and stretched. Giving his mother a quick peck on the cheek, he strapped on his mask and left the infirmary. Now hiding in the shadows, away from the Londoners, he sprinted down the tunnel and up the tall stairs.

Thomas grit his teeth and pushed the hidden door open. The tall buildings that once surrounded the area were gone; instead of a crumbled street and alleyway like before, a massive, junky hill of rubble now blocked his way. Shaking his head, he gave an exhausted sigh and clambered up the spiked pile of wires and stone and burnt furniture.

He squinted and looked above. Though the sun had not yet risen, a red and orange haze still tainted the skies. The booms and clangs and sizzles continued. The raid was not finished. The air was still hot. After scaling up and down the first mountain and hopping onto the uprooted sidewalk, Thomas rubbed his hands together and looked around. He placed a hand under his chin and tapped his foot, trying to withdraw a map from his memory.

He grumbled in disbelief. Nothing looked familiar anymore. Just as he was about to pace back and forth, he heard a sharp, faint whistling noise. He loosened the gas mask and rubbed at his ear, wondering if it was real or not. But as the birdlike sound only grew louder and stronger in volume and pitch, he frowned and threw his head back. Up, up, up in the painted sky was a blurry, dark object. And it was growing bigger and bigger and closer and closer.

Thomas whimpered. His whole body shivered. With a grunt, he leapt ahead as far as he could. His heavy feet carried him forward. He refused to look back. As he charged with great effort, he heard something that sounded like a fierce thunderclap. Far behind him, the surrounding air heated up. A wave of smoke and flames shot forth, burning any rubble that stood in its path.

Running in a zigzag pattern, poor Thomas tried his best to escape the blast. Over felled lampposts and under steel arches he went. Once he found himself cornered in between three razed building walls, he halted sharply and shifted his eyes to and fro. Though his glass goggles were fogged up by steam, he noticed that one of the structures had a large glass window and a spacious room inside. Without hesitation, Thomas plucked a rough brick from the ground and hurled it forward. The window shattered in seconds. Before the hot smoke could consume him, he dove in and ran straight ahead. Taking cover behind an upturned table, he lay on his side and covered his face. He clenched his eyes tight, waiting for another blast or wave of smog. But when neither came forward, he drew the courage to open his eyes and loosen his grip.

He did not see much at all. Every light in the large room was shut off or in pieces. Sprawled out on the ground, Thomas started to crawl away from the table to get a better look at his location. The large room was filled with thick shelves, each displaying crystalline cups and bowls and sleek figurines. A broken sign near the ceiling, now stained with black charcoal, displayed the words, 'Ye Olde Glass Shoppe'.

Thomas gasped. He sighed in relief at the homely sight. Most of the items and stands were untouched, along with the interior walls and clean flooring. For once, he felt safe and acquainted. He sniffled and gave an exhausted smile. For a few tender, quiet minutes, all was well and good.

But his respite did not last very long. As soon as he stood up, he heard a deep rumble emerge. The cold tile below his feet vibrated angrily. One by one, the coloured glass items began to fall to the ground with a shrill. Thomas winced, clumsily dodging vases and bottles and jars and frames as they struck the hard floor and broke like sharp ice. Once he heard another loud *kaboom* from outside, he sprinted towards the nearest door and ran deep into the factory.

The light from the broken windows was fading fast. Making his way around the furnaces and sandpiles and crafting tables, Thomas searched for the emergency exit. He gave a worried look and wrinkled his nose. The stillness and lack of his fellow workers felt unnatural and eerie.

He whimpered and grimaced at the thought. Once he found the steel door and pried it open, he yelped and hurried out into the burning street.

The stone road ahead sloped down in between a tight alley. Thomas leaned against the side of the glass shop to catch a quick breather. As he tried to slouch down and sit on the ground, however, a harsh battering sound came from above. He flinched and covered his head as another flaming blast struck the roof of the shop and sent bricks flying down towards him. Keeping his head covered, he bolted straight down the nearest road he could find.

<u>Chapter 4: River Thames</u>

He tried to hold back tears as he ran. His mask crawled with steamy droplets of sweat, fog, and dark stains.

For a good long while, he had followed the winding River Thames back to the centre of town where his house still stood. As he sprinted along the stone wall that divided the road from the steep drop below, he huffed and puffed, for his bones and heart had ached greatly.

He knew not what to tell his father. In his aching, pounding head, he tried to form sentences explaining his absence, the dead chief, Millie May, the underground, and so much more. Jumbled apologies swarmed in his head like flocks of dark birds. Nothing made sense. No matter how hard he wondered and thought, his vision was cloudy and his mind was sore.

He leaned against the short stone wall to catch his breath. He hadn't heard another blast within the area for quite some time. Once again, in the midst of the haze, he was alone. But then, he looked far ahead and saw where the wall arched slightly to the right.

There, Thomas saw a man. From this perspective, he resembled a mere speck in a large canvas of brick and fire and orange sky. But though he was quite far and quite lonely, he was a man all the more.

The man stood on top of a broken wall. With his back turned on the city, he faced the River Thames and turned his gaze towards its waters. Lowering his head, he stretched out his arms as far as he could.

Thomas felt his heart skip a beat. He forsook his body's sharp cries of pain and weariness. Swinging his arms back and forth as hard as he could, he charged towards the man and lunged right at him.

"No!" he screamed, grabbing the stranger by the waist. He strained and pulled back, bringing them both to the hard, cracked ground.

With a grunt, they rolled over and staggered to their feet. Ripping the mask off of his own face, Thomas looked well upon whom he had saved.

He was tired and grey, with a ripped, odorous suit and worn shoes. On his face he wore cracked spectacles that were covered by long, dirtied blonde hair. He took a step back and rasped.

Thomas nearly fell over. With his knees trembling, he covered his mouth and shook.

"Dad-" he cried. "Dad, it can't be- it can't be you...what were y-you doing...What were you-"

Thomas broke into tears. He wept and shuddered until his fingers felt numb. In the midst of it all, Edwin could not look him in the eyes. At the dark road he stared, still as the stones themselves.

"You should get...you should get inside." he muttered, barely loud enough to hear.

"Oh? And do what? Wait down below while you kill yourself?"

"It's not...it's not safe out here. Things. There are things you should not be able to see. Perhaps I am one of them!"

"No," Thomas cried, "no, you don't understand." He grabbed his father's large head and looked right into his eyes.

"Look at me." he growled. "You...you can't do this. I...I found Mum. Do you hear me? Mum is alive! Do you know how devastated she would have been if I wasn't here? Do you know what you could have done to her? To me?"

He grabbed his father by the chest and held him tighter than ever before. Though Edwin did not hug him back, he did not resist.

"I suppose," said he, "that I am sorry."

"Yes," Thomas sniffled, clenching his teeth. "but so am I."

And with that, he grabbed the whistle from his pocket and blew it hard. Edwin flinched and covered his ears as the sound cut through the foggy air. Within seconds, three wardens came around the corner, pointing at the two men near the wall. Like frantic children, they dashed with great speed. Thomas let go of the whistle and put on his mask. As the *tip-tap* of the wardens' boots grew louder, he placed a firm hand on Edwin's shoulder. For once, he knew what to say.

"I'll do it, Dad," said he, "for I can't bear to see you suffer. I'll go off and punish those wretched Germans, I will. I'll...I'll raze them to the ground and drive them away! If this is what it takes to give you peace, then I'll go out and crush those steel beasts. Only then will they ravage our city no more!"

As soon as he finished his sentence, the wardens came and surrounded them both.

"Is there a problem?" one shouted, straightening his helmet and getting into a defensive stance.

"Well, yes, and a large one, at that," Thomas answered angrily, "for this man tried to end his life. Keep him under strict watch, but bring him near his wife, Emelia Atkins. You'll find her in the infirmary. I want you to take good care of them both."

At this the wardens nodded. They grabbed Edwin by the wrists and went on their way. As they struggled to get him to walk, his spectacles were hurled off of his face and onto the road. Thomas picked them up and watched the wardens disappear into an alleyway with his father, who, with saddened eyes, gave one last look behind him.

Thomas shivered and quaked. He nearly fell over. He gently walked over to the edge of the wall as the sound of the blasts continued. Staring down at the river, he watched the reflection of the red flames ooze from the burning city. They crawled higher and higher, releasing smoke that so tainted the clouds. But what he saw next made his bones shake.

Initially, he had to look a bit closer to make sure that what he was seeing was real. Indeed, down, down below, among the soft waves, were dark, lifeless bodies. They numbered no less than twenty but varied in size and shape. In the dark they floated like rags, bouncing up and down as the current carried them far off into the beyond.

Thomas gagged. He looked away and closed his eyes tight. There was nothing to say and nothing to do. As the smell of dark blood tainted the air, he looked to the sky and wept. He held his father's spectacles so tight that the broken glass cut into his hand. But still, through the pain, he cared not, for his stark and terrible choice circled around in his head like troubled waters.

<u>Chapter 5: Health to the Company</u>

Calm winds blew to and fro as a grand ship glided over a choppy current. The cool air of the night smelled of fresh salt. The light of the moon reflected on the ocean like bright, shattered pieces of glass. And save for the crashing waves and the slight howl of the winds, there was little to no sound to be heard.

Thomas stood at the deck near the ship's rail, staring at the endless rolling hills of the sea. With one hand on his scabbard and another on the brim of his rounded steel helmet, he gazed upon the great, towering waves as they tumbled down like billowing clouds in the heavens. Looking down at the briny, he thought about the River Thames back home and shuddered at how small it seemed compared to this endless blanket of navy-blue water.

"Water," he muttered, squinting into the horizon. He repeated the word over and over and over again until he was sick of it. Soon, he grew lost in thought, thinking about water and its origins and wondering how there was so much of it in the world.

Nearly seven months had passed since the desolation of London. It was only a matter of time until the people had accepted the raids as a normal part of their lives. In the heat and the dust and the rubble they pressed, still living under the ground and telling one another to carry on and fare well. Though the dragons still attacked relentlessly, a large portion of the British population had lived to see a new year.

But the dawn of a new year had introduced a swarm of larger problems.

In these days, Mr. Hitler sent not only dragons but also foxes. Now, a particularly clever fox, who went by the name of Erwin Rommel, had devilishly cut his way into the heart of North Africa with a herd of tanks right beside him. Thus, to stop the cruel general, support groups were chosen and sent to the Libyan offensive where the battles were heated as the landscape itself.

So, of course, Thomas was not alone in this endeavour. The very ship he stood upon harboured hundreds of eager men like him. And his troopmates, or platoon if you will, who numbered no more than fifteen, were close behind. Like a band of thieves, they tip-toed up the stairs and along the railing.

"Hey," whispered the youngest of the group. "Is everyone gone?"

Thomas gave one quick glance around the deck and nodded.

"It's all clear." said he. "The crew just went inside."

The men gave a sigh of relief. In less than a minute, they scurried clumsily to the rail and glanced down at the waves below. They watched in awe as the ship cut through the bubbling foam. The group giggled at their mischief and wrapped their arms around each other.

After watching the seas for a good, long moment, a soldier with a pipe in his mouth nudged the man at his left.

"Ooh, I know!" he proposed, "We should sing a song!"

The men around him blinked.

"A song?" whispered Thomas, shivering in the cold. "Are you mad? They'll hear it and send us to bed!"

"Well, at least we can say we were able to do it. By the time they stop us, we would have already finished one tune. And it's not like the lieutenant will care. He'll gripe at us and forget about it on the morrow. Come, let us sing!"

After a bit of muttering and thinking and shuffling and nodding, the group had agreed. The bearded soldier took a deep breath and rendered the first line. Before long, the men harmoniously sang a soft tune that went something like this:

> *Kind friends and companions, come join me in rhyme*
> *Come lift up your voices in chorus with mine*
> *Come lift up your voices as we sing this refrain*
> *For we may or might never all meet here again.*

> *Here's a health to the company*
> *And one to my lass (lass!)*
> *Let us drink and be merry all out of one glass (glass!)*
> *Let us drink and be merry, as we sing this refrain*
> *For we know not (oh, we know not!) if we'll meet here again...*

Once the melody was over, a warm silence fell over the small band of infantrymen.

"I love that song." sighed the heaviest soldier, taking a swig of his drink.

"Aye, I agree," said the youngest. He put a hand under his small chin and looked up.

"Say, I just realised," he piped, "...I think that might be a good byname for us!"

The group thought for a bit and nodded with approval.

"Hmm. The Company?" replied the bearded soldier. "Not a bad fit. Quite easy to remember. What say you all?"

"Aye!" the group said in unison. Some raised their drinks in merriment while others nodded and straightened their helmets.

"But wait," Thomas deadpanned, "we be not Company-sized. There are about fifteen of us! Surely, it makes no sense."

He waited for the others to back him up. Yet still, not much was said.

"Bah," grumbled the pipe smoker. "Shut up, you. Always trying to spoil our fun. All who agree that our name be 'The Company' anyway, say 'aye' again!"

Waving their hands in the air, the other men all gave a mighty, "Aye!"

"Indeed," said the youngest. "'Tis a name with a nice, catchy ring. Behold! 'The Company, the Company!' they'll cheer. 'Godspeed to the Company! Heroes of England!'"

And with that, the men hollered with glee. With proud hearts, they belted out a strong tune that went like this:

Now we are ready to sail for the horn!
Weigh hey, roll and go.
Our boots and our clothes, boys, are all in the pawn
To be rollicking, randy dandy oh.

Heave a pawl, and heave away!
Weigh hey, roll and go.
The anchor's on board and the cables all stored
To be rollicking, randy dandy oh.

As the continuing song changed in lyric and volume, some of the men brought out their pipe lighters and sparked tiny flames in the night. Like little droplets, the scarlet lights danced and wiggled in the icy wind.

Thomas glanced over at the lighters. Before he could utter another lyric, he froze.

He grimaced at the fire and shook. His head began to spiral and his breathing began to stifle. In one of the flames, he saw Millie May in the dark. In another, he saw blazing buildings and ember roads. As the yellow wisps burned brighter and surrounded him so, he panted heavier and heavier and felt as if he were falling.

Shaking his head, he stumbled away from the group and hurried across the deck on his own. Of course, the Company, in the midst of their song, did not notice. The merry sound of their voices faded and echoed the farther he went.

In time, he had crossed the ship. Leaning heavily on the rail, he inhaled sharply and covered his face. Looking back, he wondered if anyone had seen him. Below, the waves tossed and turned, causing the ship to creak. Thomas waited and waited, catching his breath with great care. Just as he was about to turn around and head back, he noticed a tall silhouette standing at the other side.

Squinting, he tried his best to see who it was. Like the others, the figure donned a round helmet and had a slim figure. But his large carrot-like nose and slim, protruding cowlick did not look familiar at all. Straight ahead he stared, leaning against the rail as the wind blew his hair astern. Though he stood still as a stone, the reflected light of the stars and moon above danced on his shiny helmet like tiny spirits.

Before Thomas could walk over to get a closer look, he heard a cluster of angry voices. He turned around and saw some of the crewmen, running up the stairs and shining their torches and running fast across the deck. Farther ahead, the Company scattered and scrambled back to the doors.

Thomas began to sprint away. After taking a few strides, he turned his gaze towards the other side of the ship and gasped in confusion. The side of the creaking boat was now bare; the mysterious figure that once stood at the edge was now gone.

<u>Chapter 6: Strange Rumours</u>

Though it felt like weeks, the crawl across the sea lasted only a few days. Fortunately, save for a bit of rain and a few small scuffles between the ship's crew and some members of the large support group, nothing calamitous had happened on board.

Once the air had warmed and the sight of land was caught, the men quickly found out what they were going to have to deal with.

For instance, the harbour, in a way, was barely a harbour to begin with. There were no other docked ships and no pier in sight. There were no buildings or lighthouses or anything of the sort. And there were no dark rain clouds, puffing chimneys, or smog. Instead, the location of interest resembled somewhat of a wild tropical island, with swaying palm trees and small, protruding rocks.

The faint cries of seabirds pierced the skies like small sirens. The surrounding air felt warm and heavy, like a soft blanket of heat. The rustle of swaying branches echoed as the soft crashing of waves rumbled nearby. Below, the clear water dazzled with bright arctic blues and greens and whites.

The men all flocked to the edge like children, muttering mixed, muddled comments of confusion and awe. Thomas heard a hundred boots thunder towards him. Before he could sprint to the door, the hollering crowd pushed him back and dragged him to the rail.

"Ho!" he exclaimed, trying to wriggle free. "Do you all want to kill me? Move over!"

To his dismay, the throng drowned out his pleas. Sighing in discomfort, he covered his ears, stood on his toes, and looked around. Shuffling to the right, he squeezed through the small gaps in the crowd with great effort. In the meantime, two crewmen, who had kept watch on the deck, were also less excited about docking.

"Late and late again!" huffed the navigator, spying on the beach with a pair of silver binoculars. "Where are the lorries? These blokes need to get on their way."

"Oh, do calm down, you." laughed the first mate. "You're just upset that your hat was blown astern. Be patient. They'll come."

"They better! Oh, they better. I'll cut someone if they don't. If I spend one more second under this wretched sun, I'll burst. Just look at my skin! It's red as a phone box. Now move it!"

The red navigator snorted like a steamy bull and gave a violent kick to the soldier closest to him. The soldier, who just so happened to be Thomas, flew to the ground and huffed as he landed on his backside. Disorientated and quite hot, he shook his head and looked up to see an outstretched hand zip towards him. Thomas grabbed it and was hoisted up. It took him a few seconds to realise that the man who helped him up was the captain.

For weeks, the men seldom saw the captain's face. One could easily mistake him for a standard crewman with his beaked cap and dark uniform. But in this case, it was the gold buttons and Royal insignia that gave it away.

"My dear navigator!" the captain bellowed. "I assume you know better than to mistreat our escortees. What has gotten into you?"

"Well, Captain, don't look at me," argued the disgruntled navigator. "I say we leave everyone here. What say you, sir? Hm?"

At first, the captain said nothing. He then turned his large head and squinted at the jungle. As he narrowed his eyes at the glaring sunlight, his forehead and full beard dripped with fat beads of sweat. Apparently, his hat was not enough to shield him from the torridity; though he had stood outside for merely a few minutes, his fair face was already beginning to peel in the heat.

"Any second now, lads," he hushed. "Three...two..."

And with that, a thick cuboidal object had poked out of the foliage past the beach. Its light, greenish colour blended in with the vegetation around it; if it weren't for its large, dark wheels, it would have been nigh impossible to spot.

After a few seconds, a man hopped out the side and waved. Though the men on the ship could not see his facial features, they all recognised his flat, rounded helmet.

"See? No need to fret," said the captain. "Now go and wake the major general. And do get yourself some shade, mind you; I fear you've been out for far too long, young lad! Beware the heat of the sun. Someone once told me that with hot temperatures come hot temperament...or...was it with hot temperament comes hot temperatures? Oh, never mind it all. Farewell!"

After leaving the ship, Thomas and the others were shoved into the back of the lorries, which, despite being covered with tarps, still absorbed the foggy humidity that so drenched the air. The Company, of course, sat together. With eager excitement, they scrambled to their seats like hungry dogs. Poor Thomas, who was unable to catch up, sat at the very end and groaned at his discomfort.

At first, they saw nothing but green, as the vast canopy blotted out the light skies. Above, the loud *vrmm-vrmm* of the lorries' engines interrupted the songs of the colourful birds that flew to and fro. Below, the broad leaves dripped with dew, welcoming croaking frogs and scurrying mice.

It did not take long for problems to arise. As the apparent mugginess worsened, dark clouds of flies and gnats rushed into the vehicles and tormented the men greatly. At first, the poor lads grunted and yelled, slapping their own faces and shooing the bugs away. Eventually, once they realised it was all for naught, the soldiers shook their heads and tried to turn their attention towards other things.

At one point, the Company's vehicle became caught in oozing mud without warning. In the wet, claggy soil, it sputtered and screeched in vain. So, whilst the other groups waited, the men hopped out the back and grabbed at the lorry in an attempt to force it back on sturdier ground.

"One!" said the stockiest.

"Two!" said the thinnest.

"And three!" said the pipe smoker, grunting much louder than the others.

With a mighty "Heave!", the men pushed their poor vessel out of the mud and cheered as it droned on forward. With pride in their hearts, they patted each other on the shoulder and boarded once again. As soon as the vehicle went on its way, Thomas peeked his head out the back, wondering if the entire journey would look like this and naught more. But soon enough, the trees became more sparse as mud was replaced with sand and jungle became desert.

The African continent was nothing like England at all. There were no cars, no flats, no lampposts, and no paved streets. There were no clouds of any sort, either; instead, the skies were covered by a thin blanket of scintillating blue and naught more. Below, the plains seemed to stretch endlessly to the horizon and back, leaving the naked eye with nothing to see but pale sands and dark, jagged rocks. And worst of all, while the sun seldom shone upon London or Bristol, it continued to beam harshly upon these lands as if it were just a few kilometres over the ground.

For a brief moment, the quick-eyed Companyman sitting across from Thomas noticed some darting shapes in the distance. With a stutter, he called out to his comrades and pointed at the sight. The men flocked to the edge of the lorry, murmuring with intense curiosity.

There, upon the beige-coloured dunes, galloped a slim antelope. Behind it ran a pack of scrappy dogs, yipping and snarling as they snapped at the poor animal's ankles. After a short, bloodied chase, the larger animal was overpowered by its pursuers. With great haste, the wild dogs lunged forward and brought their victim to the ground.

The Companymen watched in shock and awe as the antelope was ripped apart from the backside. Some, such as the shortest and the loudest, watched the red butchery with dark fascination and described the sight in great detail. Others, such as the eldest and the quietest, covered their mouths and looked on with sad eyes.

Amid the commotion, Thomas shrunk back. One glance was enough for him. Whilst the others gazed at the slaughter, he turned away and shivered until the lorry had driven far past the gruesome spectacle.

For the rest of the day, some of the men told stories of their early years and their friends and their towns. It all began when the youngest, the most curious of the group, asked the pipe smoker why he lived and breathed in his own cloud of tobacco.

"Well, humf," the pipe smoker replied, "for I was a proud barkeeper for many, many moons. After years of sampling brandy and gin, I could nearly taste the day of my retirement. But nay! It was taken from me in mere moments, for the draft called for sad, able-bodied men without fear. 'Go slay dragons!' they said, 'For now, you will live without a single thought of your lovers and kin.'"

As he went to light his pipe with stark aggression, the eldest chuckled.

"Oh, hush," laughed he. "Yes, do lighten up. You're free to think of your kin as often as you'd like, as they bring more warmth and cheer than your smokes ever will. I myself have two darling children aged fourteen and ten. As of now, they live in the West Country, frolicking in the footsteps of a schoolmaster and receiving the finest education of all."

Before he could ramble some more, the youngest raised his hand and spoke up.

"Finest education! Well, sir, I'm glad you brought that matter to the table. For I attended a Catholic school for two years and a boarding school for three! I know everything about kings and prophets and creatures and plants. And most of all, I know, oh I know, that we'll win this fight, lads!"

And so, once they had run out of true stories to share, they began to tell tall tales and more speculations about the war itself. Late in the evening, when the air was cool, the youngest opened up the discussion.

"I heard some news," said he, wobbling to and fro as the vehicle hit some rocks on the road. "Yes, good news indeed!"

The others leaned in and tilted their heads. Huddling together, they looked on with childlike interest and excitement.

"Indeed," he continued, "you all know how the groups here are to assist the tank crews and fight alongside them?"

"Indeed!" piped the others, nodding their heads.

"Well, apparently, we're in luck. For British tanks are nigh invincible."

"I-invincible?" said the jumpiest, cocking his head.

"Yes, indeed! Invincible. The tank crews we're helping are cunning and strong. Once we are assigned to ours, they will show us their ways and teach us their methods."

With the exception of Thomas, who was listening silently, the group gasped and mumbled and cheered.

"Wait, but there's more!" the youngest continued. "See, a cousin of mine in another group heard from a friend's uncle's neighbour of his. I don't recall the name that was said, but the staff sergeant that we're helping is some sort of hero."

"Hero?"

"Aye, hero. He's a fearless one, I've heard! And a master of plans, they said. He's got a keen eye and sharp knowledge of the land. And not to mention that he has medals and badges galore. I heard that once, he faced the Fox head-on and sent him running to the hills. He's got tens - no - hundreds! Of great tanks by his side!"

Thus, on the second day, they talked about the tanks once more.

"Somelad told me," said the youngest, "that they're the fastest on Earth. Faster than anything the Germans can throw at us!"

"If so, do you think," asked the pipe smoker, straightening his helmet, "that we'll be able to man some of those mighty vehicles?"

The men chuckled to one another and grinned.

"Oh, no doubt!" said the youngest. "In time, we'll be experts. For we'll be instructed by England's bravest, hardiest, and most quick-witted souls! We'll blast through walls and brigades, with the sturdiest vessels and sturdiest men!"

On the third day, of course, they spoke of the men.

"Haven't you heard?" said the youngest. "Aye, the men be strong! They're like a tight unit, they are. Closer together than we! I heard that they can take at least three bullets a day each. Yet, they'd go great lengths to save one another. Perhaps, oh perhaps! We'll be braver than they!"

With strength in their hearts, the men grinned and whooped and shared some more tales. And for hours and hours, they continued to babble and laugh without a care in the world.

<u>Chapter 7: The Saint</u>

The air was especially clear at this time. The thin clouds above had vanished or floated into the distance. Though the sun and its heat had retreated, the frigid winds and icy gusts now took their place. And thus, the men built homely campfires to protect themselves from the cold.

Night had approached. Whilst the other platoons in the area were asleep in their tents, the Company huddled around the fire and watched. Of course, the only exception was Thomas, who sat close behind in his group's empty lorry with a bugle at his side. The sight of the campfire was too much to bear. Trembling slightly, he grasped a thin blanket and draped it across his shoulders. In the dark and the cold he remained, waiting and waiting for the night to be over.

When the sound of crackling flames became too repetitive, the topic of strange beasts had arisen. It started when the tallest soldier, a rather confident soul, asked his peers,

"If there were a dragon roaming these lands, what colour do you think it would be? Do state your case. For I am a curious fellow."

Of course, the others did not know what to say. They all looked to the sky and furrowed their brows.

"Perhaps it is green like a snake." one suggested, shrugging his shoulders.

"Perhaps, perhaps! But not all snakes are green," another argued. "Some live in the sands and are, therefore, quite brown. So, I think the dragons are brown."

"No, no, no. You are both in the wrong," grumbled the oldest soldier, scratching his chin. "If the dragon were to hide up in the skies, it might as well be blue and white to match. Nobody would ever suspect a blue dragon!"

"Oh," huffed the pipe smoker, "and I suppose we should not waste our breath. I don't believe there are dragons where we are going, anyway!"

And with that, the men started to bicker. In a matter of minutes, each one was now getting up and turning to his neighbour and arguing why his side was right and the other was wrong. What was once a pool of discussion was now an energised, heated debate chock full of yelling and grumbling and swinging of arms. And it did not seem like it was going to stop.

But what happened next was rather surprising.

"Aye," uttered a sibylline voice, silencing the loud hoard of grumblers. "There are, indeed, dragons in Libya."

The men turned around in an instant. Some instinctively grasped their rifles and knives while others stepped back and nearly fell over. Upon hearing the faint sound of footsteps, they all looked to their right and saw a tall form creep forward from behind the rocks.

The orange glow of the fire revealed the detailed attributes of the figure's face. He had a long, triangular nose and baggy eyes. His uniform was tauny, greenish, and well-kept. Atop his head lay a glistening helmet with a white, painted circle and a red cross at its middle. Below it was a receded tuft of auburn hair. And strangely enough, the man carried no weapon.

Thomas squinted a little, wondering why this man looked so familiar. After a bit of thinking, he suddenly remembered and gasped quietly.

The man on the ship! he thought.

Quite puzzled, he turned to his neighbour to whisper a question. But that's when the medic spoke up.

"You all know the tale...but perhaps you don't recall." said he.

"Aye, long ago, there was a village in the Libyan desert. Surrounding it was a sparkling river that gave the people all that they needed. In the heat of the day and the cool of the night, the town prospered; under the peaceful rule of the king and his young daughter, all seemed like paradise. But one day, without warning, a dragon approached the village and roared mightily! With its breath, it poisoned the river and all who drank from it perished in minutes. Like a merciless conqueror, it claimed the riverside and the fields and the forest for itself and devoured all who came near. Now, to-"

"Rubbish!" interrupted the pipe-smoking soldier. "Rubbish and gash! I suppose we're in no mood or mindset to talk about fairy tales like huddled children, are we?" he huffed.

In response, the doctor glared at him without blinking. The flames from the campfire danced in the reflection of his glassy, blue eyes. The other men stood still as stones and looked back at their companion helplessly, waiting for the medic to bestow some ill or mysterious punishment upon him. But still, nothing happened, for the tall figure just continued to stare and stare without saying a word.

The pipe smoker looked away and remained silent, turning beet red from shame, terror, and a balanced combination of both.

"Now, as I was saying," hissed the medic, "to prevent the dragon from devastating the village with fire, the people offered it a sheep each morning. This seemed to satiate the beast for some time. But alas, once they had run out of sheep, the villagers reluctantly began to sacrifice their own children. Indeed, every child under the age of twenty would be tied up and thrown into the wilderness, never to be seen again. To do this, their melancholic king would wake up quite early, pull a name out of a box, and announce who the unlucky suitor would be. And after days and days of this awful routine, it was time for the king to finally sacrifice his own daughter to the dragon."

Upon hearing this, the men gasped and started to mutter.

"But hearken, for there was hope after all! For a brave knight by the name of Saint George came riding his steed in search of some water. When he saw the princess bound to a tree, he rode up without thought and came to her aid. Once the dragon came storming forward, the Saint drew his weapon and yelled furiously. With divine rage, he tied up the beast, brought it to the village square, and cut off its head with one clean swing of his mighty sword."

The men gasped in excitement at the end of the tale. They whistled and cheered and shook their rifles in the air like children watching a grand film.

"And so," said the medic, raising a brow, "to answer your other enquiry, no matter what colour a dragon may be, it will always be red. Indeed, it wears the blood of its victims on its armoured scales just as you wear those boots on your feet."

But the Company was not listening anymore. For now they stood tall, unsheathing their weapons and yelling, "Huzzah!"

"A heroic tale," cried they, "with a strong, dashing ending! Do you hear that, lads? We'll be like Saint George! We'll slay those metal beasts and all will know of our names!"

In response, the medic scowled and crossed his thin arms.

”You fools!” he scolded. "Will you not heed my warning? Surely, I tell you! There be a beast in these lands!”

Still, his cries fell on deaf ears. Shaking his head, he turned around and marched in the direction from whence he came. The only one who noticed him leave was Thomas, who had watched and heard everything from the lorry's edge. Now lying on his side, he held his blanket tighter and fell into a deep sleep.

<u>Chapter 8: The Dream</u>

Thomas was enveloped by hollow emptiness. It was not an eerie darkness found in a frightening cave or an abandoned house or a bottomless trench down in the briny deep; instead, it was a calm, cool, pitch-black place filled with silence and crisp, clean air. Here, there was no quarreling or hurrying or any ill danger. Though he still wore that steel helmet and pale uniform, he grasped no weapon and felt no fear.

Walking forward, he heard no sound save for the quiet *click-clack* of his own footsteps. The ground beneath his shoes felt rough and craggy, like some sort of stone road. And then he saw a light.

It was small and faded. Far and ahead he squinted, trying to investigate who or what was behind it. But the light grew fast in size and intensity; within seconds, it transformed into a thin beam of fire. Barreling forward it went, filling the cool air with a strong wave of heat.

Thomas dodged the beam just in time. He jumped sideways, covering his head and neck as he divebombed to the ground below. As he landed with a clumsy *thump*, he cringed as his elbow and side felt battered and bruised.

And then he looked up and grimaced once more.

Right above him soared a red dragon, spewing fire upon the ground a few metres ahead. From this angle, he could see the beast's tightly-knit scales and chipped, yellow fangs. On its horned face were thin, beardlike spikes that rattled as the wind flew past it.

The beast came like a hurricane. Each flap of its tattered, batlike wings sent a gust of wind crashing down below. With a loud *whoosh,* a torrent of smoke, sand, and ash shot forward in large, hot clouds.

Thomas covered his ears as the dragon let out a piercing, unholy screech. It sounded somewhat like a lion and somewhat like an eagle. As the beast spewed more flame and sulfur, the light from the blast rapidly pushed aside the darkness and illuminated the ground below it. Looking up, Thomas saw stone buildings and streets. He cowered at its familiarity.

To his right was a charred, broken sign with the Royal Mail service emblem. Around it were the same scattered heaps of wood and concrete that once held the small building in place.

To his left snaked the thick stone parapet that barred the streets from the River Thames.

"No, no, not again." he choked, grasping his face and breathing heavily. "Not again, not again, not again…"

Empty cars and piles of wreckage shined in the smoky, infernal atmosphere. The air, which was heavy with smoke, billowed as far as the eye could see. Thomas pushed himself off of the ground and ducked as a large shadow flew over him. Wide-eyed, he ran as far as he could towards the river and followed its path. As he went around the winding path and hopped up and down the crooked stairs, he noticed a thin object leaned against the wall far ahead. Curious, he ran faster; as he came closer and saw its wooden frame and slender shape, he recognised it as his rifle and snatched it gracefully.

A weapon! Surely the dragon did not stand a chance. Thomas slung the gun over his shoulder. By the riverside he charged, feeling very exhausted but light on his feet.

He cocked his head, looking for the highest point of elevation. In his line of sight, he saw a white domed building with a steel balcony. Upon it was a bell tower and a fluttering Union Jack. It stood just as high as the dragon flew. Thomas halted and ran in its direction.

Up a mountain of rubble he climbed. Sometimes, his foot would slip and his hand would scrape, making the trek all the more difficult. But despite these discomforts, he clambered on and on until he finally reached the tippy-top.

Pouncing onto the balcony, he cocked his rifle and pointed it forward. From this view, he had a better look. The bell behind him swung and chimed angrily. Though Thomas listened for any sign of the dragon's whereabouts, he heard nothing else. The beast was missing. Something was wrong.

"W-well? Show yourself!" he exclaimed, cupping his left hand over his mouth. Still nothing. This couldn't be. He felt his heart start to pound louder and louder as if it were trying to burst out of his chest. The air was still, and the dragon was nowhere to be found.

Then, like a typhoon, the beast shot up from below, scraping its body, wings, and tail against the building's side. Pieces of stone and glass showered everywhere in large chunks as the structure shook. Thomas almost fell over but caught himself on the railing. He then bit his lip and watched the dragon ascend higher and higher until it looked as small as a bird.

At first, it was so far away that it seemed like it was going to disappear. But as soon as it reached the clouds, it turned back around and dove straight towards the dome.

Down, down, down it went. As it descended, it seemed to get bigger and bigger. And as it opened its jaws, its throat lit up with bright orange flames. Thomas clenched his teeth, anticipating the blast. There was no time to waste. He pointed the gun straight up as the beast plummeted down. Closing one eye, he aimed right for the dragon's mouth as it came closer and closer.

And then he pulled the trigger.

Bang.

Just as he shot, the dragon spewed out molten fire. Thomas covered his face with his forearms as the thin cyclone of flames spiraled right into him. And then, all went black.

Thomas inhaled sharply as he woke up. He sat up and rubbed his hot face. Squinting, he took notice of the lorry's tarp roof and hard seats. He sighed in relief and stared out the back.

"I suppose," he sobbed, grasping whatever he could, "that slaying a dragon is nothing like making glass."

<u>Chapter 9: The Rats</u>

Thomas woke up with great difficulty the next morning. He had gotten up and fallen back asleep at least three or four times that night. His helmet, which had been strapped around his head, covered his face almost completely. He scrounged the camp for something to eat and drink. But once he learnt that there was nothing left, he frowned and complained as he boarded the lorry with the others.

The long-nosed medic entered the cabin of the vehicle. He sat in the passenger seat, turned to the driver, and quietly mentioned that this would be the Company's last day on the road. While this news proved to be somewhat encouraging, Thomas's mood did not get any merrier. Once again, he was placed at the very end, facing the sun and the sand as the journey continued.

It did not take long for the Company to feel quite hot and irritated as well. When the repeating sight of the landscapes made their eyes tired and sore, they started to find amusement within each other. For instance, their lieutenant, who was a young, confident lad who had fallen asleep for most of the journey, had a rather odd quirk; for some reason, every twenty minutes or so, he needed to take a short leak off the edge. The Company, laughing behind their palms, tried to predict each time he would do it and secretly decided to give him the byname 'Lieutenant Bladders' along the way.

Later, the attention was on Thomas. At midday, he opened his shirt pocket and fetched a pair of spectacles from its case. The glass lenses were carefully removed but the frames remained. Regardless, he placed them upon his nose bridge and gently pushed them towards his face. It wasn't a bad fit, but they gently bounced up and down each time the lorry hit a bump on the road. This sudden change in movement, however, easily attracted the attention of his companions, who turned to him and stared with tilted heads and shifty eyes.

"What is it?" said Thomas, breaking the silence.

"Well, that's just what I was about to ask you." stated the pipe smoker, who sat on the bench across from him. "What be that?"

"Why, they're...spectacles." Thomas deadpanned. "Surely you've seen some before."

"And why do you wear them? It ruins the way you look."

"Humpf! I can see just fine, thank you."

At this, the Company laughed.

"That helmet on too tight?" jested the quick-eyed infantryman sitting next to the pipe smoker. He poked Thomas's chest with a thin, crooked finger. "You're the only one among us who wears a necktie, after all. What's wrong, chum? Maybe you forgot that we're going to a battleground and not a schoolground! Eh, Specs?"

This made the men whoop even harder. Snorting at his companions in disdain, Thomas silently swiped the spectacles from his face and wiped them clean with his tie. Looking away, he rubbed his nail over the light etchings on the frame's side.

At first glance, they were near indistinguishable. But to a trained eye, it was clear that they spelt the name 'Edwin Atkins' in elegant cursive. He read the name in his head and sighed lightly, thinking about his father and mother both trapped in the underground back home. He quietly watched the sky for hours, fixating on the colours as they changed from baby blues to neon oranges to deep, violet hues.

This particular day of travel seemed to last longer than the others. One man claimed that he spotted a plane in the distance, but such a thing was never proven true. Another said that he saw a boxcar stuck in the dunes, but that was quickly dismissed as well. After more and more false allegations, the men concluded that the strong heat started to welcome strange illusions. But still, the Company remained alert and ready in case something were to actually happen.

Eventually, the major general gave a signal, and the other lorries halted near a sandy grove of tall trees. The Company's vehicle, however, drove onward without turning to the left or to the right. Thomas watched as the general nodded to the driver and the lonely medic before turning around and tending to other matters.

"Wait," Thomas murmured, "where are we going? The others already convened at the stop. What in the world is going on?"

"Ah, shut up again!" growled the pipe smoker. "Perhaps, we'll meet up with some others. Surely, this is part of the plan, it is! Just you wait."

"I agree," said the big-eared Companyman. "What, do you think the War Ministry would blindly march us to our deaths? Perhaps, we'll join an even bigger unit of men."

"I still don't like this one bit." Thomas grumbled, getting out of his seat. "Something here seems rather unprofessional. Off-putting, even! We should stop the lorry. Driver! Stop the lorry! Stop the-"

But before he could say another word, the other Companymen grabbed him and placed him back where he belonged. With great shame, he looked away and said nothing more.

In time, all became still as the Company's lone vehicle halted behind a sea of large dunes. At first, the men thought they had run out of petrol. They looked towards the rear end, urging Thomas to take a peep out the back and report anything that showed up.

Thomas swiveled around, feeling the hair on his back stand up. At first, he saw nothing particularly different; if anything, the ground on the landscape was hardened and the sand piles were smaller and flatter. He narrowed his eyes and shrugged.

"It's nothing, really. All I see is-"

But before he could finish, a large boxlike shadow seemed to pass by. The Company cowered and exclaimed all at once. Some hid behind whoever was in front of them. Others just froze and stuck out their limbs like stiff trees.

Thomas glanced behind to see the object. It had a tannish colour and bright, metal shine. On its top sat a lengthy cannon that protruded forward. Below, it had a set of long, ridged tracks that wound around great wheels like a belt in a factory. And though it glimmered in the bright sun, its armoured hide remained somewhat covered in sand and mud as if it were a piece of the earth itself.

"Is it our own?" whimpered the youngest, shaking in his boots.

"We're not dead, so it must be!" Thomas exclaimed. Before he could say anything else, the tank had ceased.

"By Jove," gasped the youngest. "So it is true! We're here!"

At this, the Company cheered in unison. With marvelous speed, they leapt out of the vehicle and sprinted excitedly towards the encampment. Unbeknownst to them, the lonely medic shook his head as he watched. Sitting quite comfortably in the lorry's front seat, he turned to the Company and called out to them.

"Hmf!" he shouted, "Farewell and goodbye, brave heroes of England! I'm off to aid a much wiser division. Good luck and good health to your doctors and friends!"

Meanwhile, upon arrival, the Company stood in a straight line. With their rifles slung across their backs, they stared straight ahead and fidgeted slightly. Thomas, who stood somewhere in the middle, took a step back to maintain some distance from the others around him. While they waited, Lieutenant Bladders excused himself briskly. He nodded to the group, rushed over to the tank, and disappeared behind it.

The Company stared at the greenish tents a few metres across. The flaps in the front fluttered in the wind like the wings of a butterfly. At first glance, it looked like the structures numbered around ten. Thomas squinted and wondered how many there really were. Looking down, he kicked at the ground. The sand beneath his feet felt firm and warm and looked like red clay. Sighing, he tilted his head up and looked at the sun with half-lidded eyes. Though his helmet protected his head and neck from burning, he still continued to sweat quite profusely. In all this discomfort, he frowned and tapped his foot several times.

After about two minutes, a hand popped out from one of the tents. As it pulled the flap back, the Company saw a man peek outside.

"Oi, they're here!" he called out in a gruff, singsongy voice.

"They're here?" shouted another man, peeking next to him. "Aye, aye! Jolly good! Indeed, they are! Come, let us wager!"

And with that, a few trios of soldiers zoomed out of the tents and ran forward. Their stomping, which stirred up red clouds of sand and dust, sounded like soft thunder.

Once they clustered together a metre away from the Company's line, they did something rather unexpected; reaching into their pockets, they withdrew papers and pencils and dice and started to examine their guests.

The Company took a few steps back, stared with puzzled eyes, and began to mutter to one another. Thomas, however, was busy looking at the uniforms.

The strangers wore tan shirts, shorts, and high socks. They had worn neckties and carried sheathed daggers at their hips. Some donned ugly scars while others had torn, folded sleeves. Their shoulder flashes stood out as well; each man had a brown patch on his shoulder with an embroidery of a red mouselike creature standing on its hind legs.

But what caught Thomas's attention the most were the steel helmets. Though about half of them did not wear one, those who did had one that was dented, chipped, punctured, or cracked. Before Thomas could imagine what kind of battles had warranted such damage, one of the taller men pointed straight at him.

"Arr yar!" he laughed, "That one might last a week. What say you, Barkley?"

His stocky moustached companion, who was aggressively jotting something down on a notepad, shook his head.

"Tsk, tsk, tsk. I wouldn't put your hopes up, dear Trev." said he. "Why, he has spectacles! I'd wager half a pound on his head but no more."

"Well, humf! Better than the bowlegged one at the very end!" roared the broad-shouldered soldier standing next to Trev. "The Fritzes will snap him in half, they will. Once they've finished with the older one over there, at least. I'll lay odds that he'll be gone in four days' time."

The eldest in the Company heard the insult loud and clear but did not retaliate; silent as usual, he gave a warm smile. The tallest of the Company, however, stepped forward and scowled.

"Half a pound? Four days' time?" he complained. "What do you mean by that? I'm sure you know better."

But no matter how much he protested, the men sneered and scribbled and tossed their dice. Not a single member of the Company was spared from the ridicule; their oppressors continued to point and count and shout methodically like auctioneers at a county fair.

Before long, the pipe smoker lost his patience.

"What kind of introduction is this?" he hissed. "Am I to assume I'm fighting alongside the wrong men? How dare you! What is this behaviour? Where is your leader? I do believe he's our leader now too, so go spill!"

"I see you're a smart one," chuckled Barkley, twirling his dark curled moustache and folding a piece of paper. "Better put that to good use. The staffie is in his quarters, as per usual. I'll go fetch him."

The men watched Barkley turn around and prance away. When he returned, a much taller fellow marched closely behind. Once the stranger laid his eye on the Company and stood right in front of them, everyone had quieted down and looked up.

He had a slender yet strong build. His thin face donned a slight stubble and a short, umber tuft of hair that peaked at the top. A dark eyepatch, stained by dust and worn out by time, strung around his head and covered his left eye. His tattered clothes, stained with a white chalky substance, looked wholly unusual; instead of a military-issued uniform, he wore a blue cuffed longcoat with poorly-stitched badges and gold buttons. His steel helmet, which dangled over his head in a loose and crooked manner, was coloured navy blue to match.

In his left hand, he held a long, chipped pipe. In his right, he held a bottle. With his teeth, he pulled out the cork, spat it out on the ground, and took a long swig. When he finished, he wiped his mouth and stared at the Company.

"What are these, frycooks?" he boomed. His thick Bristolian accent pierced the air and seemed to catch some of the Companymen off guard. In response, Barkley cleared his throat.

"Er, no," he grumbled. "They're our new reinforcements. Did you not receive a message?"

The staff sergeant blinked thrice and looked down the bottle.

"No message in here. Whoever's in charge needs to take a walk."

The Companymen frowned and looked at each other in confusion. With their hands behind their backs, they waited uncomfortably until the section leader spoke again.

"My name is Mr. Covington," said he, "and I see ye already met my loyal crew of Rats here. Why, there be fifteen thousand tank Rats in these deserts. But my crew and I are different. We made a deal with the War Ministry, and now, we choose to go off alone. Why? Go on. Somelad ask me why."

After some awkward silence, the youngest spoke up.

"Wh-"

"Why?" Mr. Covington interrupted. "Why, to catch a Fox, of course! Ye need not an army to do it. Only a mere group of hunters. And that, my friends, be us."

As Mr. Covington continued to speak, Thomas turned to his neighbours and gave the cuckoo sign. The men next to him nodded in rapid succession.

"A Fox's bite is seldom shallow," the staff sergeant continued. "Ask me how I know. Go ask."

This time, the pipe smoker tried to respond.

"H-"

"How?" Mr. Covington interrupted again. "Because he shot me, that's how!"

He grabbed the bottom of his tan collared shirt and pulled it upward. There, on his bare, white chest, creased a jagged, maroon line with a dark depression in the middle.

Most of the Company turned away and grunted at the sight. They covered their faces, cringing and wincing and retching away. Surely, they've seen bullet wounds. But none like this.

"Aye, he did," said the staffie, scowling long and hard. "And a bloody good shot it was. But now, I wish to poke a hole through that Fox myself! And after that, I'll grab him by the tail and hang his coat on my mantle. So that, me lads, be why ye are here."

Without hesitation, he withdrew a small, silver-blue pistol and pointed it forward. As the Company gave more confused looks, Mr. Covington pulled down his shirt and started to march up and down between the two lines of men. Twirling the gun in his hand, he looked at each and every one of them in the eye.

"Now," he continued, "I should warn ye that the Fox has many servants. One of them be a ruthless wyrm that roams these lands and searches for Rats to devour. Aye, ye can say that he takes the form of a man. But nay! He be a wicked, wicked beast that spits fire and burns all in his path. Perhaps a member of our previous reinforcement team will tell ye. Bring him here, Lance Corporal."

He gave a sharp whistle and out came Barkley, holding what looked like a torn blanket. But once he threw it to the ground, the Company saw that it was not a blanket at all. Forward it rolled, leaving a nasty smell in the air. As the black cloth tumbled in the sand, a scorched helmet and dark pile of charred bones spilt forward.

Thomas and the others took a step back and groaned in horror. Some buried their faces in their shirts while others closed their eyes tight. One of them turned away and vomited on the ground a little. But even that did not stop Mr. Covington from giving his speech.

"The good news be that as a crew, we protect one another. Even from dragons." said he. "So, because I be a good, sane staffie, I will tell ye my three rules here in the desert."

One by one, he held up his fingers to count.

"If ye see a Nazi, bring him to justice. If ye see a Fox, bring him to me. And if ye see a serpent, bring him to Hell!"

Now, the Rats, still behind Mr. Covington, all lifted their weapons and cheered. The Company, however, with puzzled and miserable looks on their faces, just nodded.

"I suppose I should learn all of your names," Mr. Covington uttered, twirling the gun one more time before putting it away, "but for now, I'm busy learning this map!"

From his pocket, he pulled a rather large piece of tan parchment paper. On its face it had a faded map of the North African front, complete with a compass and a legend. But around its sophisticated printed borders and text were incomprehensible ink notes and X's and wobbly lines. The emptier spots, primarily in the desert areas and mountains, had messy drawings of winged beasts and giant squids and other strange, cruel organisms.

Before the Company could even attempt to study it more, Mr. Covington rolled it up and stuffed it in his coat.

"I want two men armed at every quadrant," he ordered. "Have the other half rest so they can take the night watch. Step lively, gentlemen! You'll see me when I say it's time to go."

And with that, the staff sergeant turned his back and marched off to his tent. The Company, who now stood in a rather crooked line, stared ahead with pure disbelief. A few of them attempted to escape back to the lorry, only to find that, to their horror, that ship had already sailed. Before any of them could utter another word, the Rats grinned and came forward and split the group in two.

<u>Chapter 10: The Lance Corporal</u>

It turned out that the Rats had assigned Thomas to the night watch. The first half of the Company, now divided into four pairs, guarded the Rats' territory and machinery and living space. The task, which lasted a few hours, was simple enough for a child to do; if a lone German or a tank or a vehicle approached, each infantryman and his companion had to sound the bugle to alert the others or fight if need be.

The Rats' encampment stood atop a grainy cliff that reached nearly nine metres from bottom to top. The open, rocky floor below, which Mr. Covington named 'The Locker', housed a plethora of scattered, thorned bushes and towering, red stones. The bluff did not look very dangerous; if a man were to roll down the side, he would acquire some bumps and bruises but would still get up without fail.

The cliffs surrounded the Locker like some sort of bowl; though it had a wide opening at the entrance and some gaping holes in the walls, few living things came into view. All throughout this rather uninteresting task, Thomas decided to find ways to entertain himself. For one hour, he practised pointing his rifle at the Locker below. For the next, he tried to count the grains of sand in his palm. And once that became boring, he looked up at the stars and tried to form constellations out of them.

He had no companions to converse with. Since the men were few in number, they were greatly spread out along the cliff and left alone in the dark. For three long nights this went on, with no action, no change, and no enemy.

Aside from the stirring of the sands, the only movement they saw was that of the desert foxes. Down in the Locker they dashed, chasing after mice and lizards and other small creatures. As they peeked out of their holes, Thomas watched them with great curiosity, pointed his rifle at them, and pretended to shoot.

Each night, Thomas and six other Companymen of the night watch were summoned to the medical tent. One by one, the lads had their scalps and eyes checked for bugs, boils, and other foul things.

The tent was dimly lit by some lanterns. In the corners were chipped, stained boxes and dull jars filled with blankets and paper. Each time, the men huddled together, sitting on coarse mats on the ground while waiting in line for the inspections. Meanwhile, Thomas always sat on a crate in the corner facing the wall, as the sight of the flames made him flinch.

The Rats' medic's name was Dr. Marion Mulbourey. He had hair as dark as wood and arms that were just as tough. It was a miracle that he could fit into the tent at all; with his tall figure and large build, he sometimes knocked over boxes and syringes without knowing. And unlike the lonely, carrot-nosed medic at the campfire before, his voice was boisterous and loud.

"Bah!" he would say as he stacked his paperwork into piles. "You blokes be in very bad shape. I wish I could do more with what was given to me. Rusted tools and rusted men. No civilization for kilometres on end. Curse these far lands! Curse these dunes. Curse these Rats, and curse the War Ministry!"

Of course, the seven Companymen in his care chuckled and nodded. With shifting eyes and stiff backs, they tried to say as little as possible for fear that the medic would lose his temper. The youngest, however, looked like he was about to burst into tears.

"Why?" he asked, tilting his head. "In all my years of schooling, I've always heard such wondrous things about the War Ministry. I thought your crew was the greatest. What went wrong, dear sir? What went wrong?"

Dr. Mulbourey cursed under his breath and kicked into the crate nearest to him.

"Well," he grumbled, struggling to free his boot from the dismantled pile of wood, "it all happened when Mr. Covington first went mad, of course."

The small band of Companymen looked at one another in great concern. Meanwhile, Thomas tilted his head to the side to get a better listen.

"How d-did it happen at all?" asked the jumpiest, "How did he g-go mad?"

"The incident!" Dr. Mulbourey exclaimed, making some of the men shake. "Happened but a few months ago. He couldn't take a shot from the Fox and wake up the same. Aye, he was a-howlin' and a-terrorizin' the nurses, going on and on about how he wanted to skewer that Nazi and set him ablaze. On some nights, he'd steal maps and scribble all over 'em. On others, he'd pace back and forth, scratching up the tent walls and a-growlin' like some sort of beast."

Thomas gasped and shivered at the idea. In mere seconds, he remembered the wild dogs tearing apart the gazelle limb from limb. Shuddering and retching at the thought of blood, he shrunk back in his seat and crossed his arms in discomfort.

"Eventually," the doctor continued, "one of us injected him with a great deal of strange medicine. So, one morning, he woke up in the middle of the night, screaming about how he's a pirate and all! Now, after many complaints from his comrades and doctors, the major general thought it'd be best to ship him back to England and have a talk with the War Ministry. A rather strange, shadowy panel of men, they are. All dressed up in their fancy suits, they spent hours thinking of ways to punish old Covington for his madness. Finally, the most loyal of the group, who went by the name of Sir Phil Anders, considered sending old Covington to the loon ward to have his brain picked at. But you wouldn't believe what happened next, you won't!"

At this point, the soldiers had scooted over so close to the doctor that they could all smell the powder in his hair.

"In the midst of his own defense," he continued, "old Covington had some rather...intense suspicions about Sir Anders. All day and all night, he pointed his bruised-up finger to the lad and said, 'By the patch on my face, I swear, that man there is a captain of the Reich!'"

The Companymen gasped at the statement.

"As expected," said Mulbourey, "the minister grew very upset. He told his comrades over and over that this allegation was false, and that Mr. Covington would stay in the loon ward until his beard turned grey. So, to shut them both up, the rest of the ministry decided that a thorough investigation was necessary. After seeing Sir Anders angrier than usual, the other lads soon latched on to the suspicions! They searched through Sir Anders's mail, office, bed, and bread, and after hunting, gathering, poking, and clawing...they found letters which proved that the great and loyal Sir Anders..."

"-was cheating on his wife!" a gnarly voice spat.

The Companymen jumped as the tent flaps flew open. Through them stormed Lance Corporal Barkley, holding a cracked flask of rum.

"Aye," he grumbled, staggering as he walked, "Mr. Covington had shed light upon a scandal, for the War Ministry found some letters that Sir Anders had exchanged with his mistress! The next day, with his face bright red and his marriage ruined, Sir Anders set his sights on Mr. Covington. He grabbed the staff sergeant by the coat and said, 'By the patch on your face, I swear, you ruined the life of a great man! To the desert with you! If killing the Fox is your wish, then I shall grant it true!'"

At this, the soldiers reacted differently. The youngest and the stoutest chortled giddily, slapping their thighs and rolling onto the ground. The jumpiest gave a nervous chuckle as the tallest and the shortest whispered to one another. The pipe smoker rolled his eyes while muttering curses under his breath, and Thomas, who remained still, thought about how ridiculous the entire story sounded.

"What's so funny about this?" Barkley growled. "We're marooned! Stuck here in the middle of nowhere in some sort of formal exile....with naught but scrapped vehicles and scrapped weapons!"

Just as he was about to stomp towards the laughing Companymen, Dr. Mulbourey stood in between.

"Again and again, Mr. Barkley," he sighed. "Didn't I tell you to lay off the drinking? It's bad for your liver and your soul."

The lance corporal gave the medic a rather bitter, ugly look.

"You can't tell me what I can and cannot drink, Doctor," he hissed, "and I do know that these men best be on their way out.

After taking a very long swig, he threw the bottle at Dr. Mulbourey's feet. Stalking towards the tent flaps, he looked back at the group one last time.

"Aye, I should warn you," he continued, "that the night watches us with cold, silver eyes."

<u>Chapter 11: Bush and Flame</u>

One night, the Company's lieutenant woke up and went out to relieve himself. When he grabbed a lantern and opened the flap of his tent, he saw Mr. Covington's great Cromwell tank on the horizon. Mesmerised by the vehicle, he put on his boots and scurried behind it.

He waited a while and marveled at the Cromwell's tracks, armour, and cannon. Once he finished, he picked up his light and wheeled around. To his surprise, he saw a tall man halt in front of him. On his head sat a glistening, quadrate helmet. In his hands he held a knife and a cone-shaped object. Behind and around him stood two others who wore the same dark coats and slick, curved boots.

For a few seconds, they stared at each other in fright. The lieutenant, being a rather skittish fellow, recognised the German-style uniforms and fumbled with his belongings. Grabbing the bugle from his side, he blew it once and produced a sharp sound that resonated all through the camp. In response, one of the intruders withdrew a handgun and shot the poor man until he was dead.

The nearby guards yelled and pointed their rifles at the oncoming threat. By the light of the lanterns, they ran towards the Cromwell and took aim.

One of the Rats shot the tallest trespasser in the face. He dropped all he had and fell within seconds. The remaining two drew their weapons and tried to fire back.

The first guard to take damage was Barkley, who roared and fell when a stray shot grazed his shoulder.

"Leave it!" he snarled, pushing away anyone who tried helping him up. "Keep firing! I don't care who you hit!"

As a bullet nearly hit his head, he got up and staggered behind his own men. Soon, Dr. Mulbourey was summoned to scout for the wounded. Without hesitation, Barkley grabbed him and flung him towards the approaching foes. Unarmed and wholly unprotected, he was shot in the middle by a German who had aimed for Trev.

Of course, at this moment, Thomas was too far from the commotion to do anything. As soon as he heard the bugle and the shouting, he grasped his rifle, stood up from the edge of the cliffside, and sprinted towards the fight. There was, however, quite a distance; in order to even get to the Cromwell, he had to pass through the whole encampment first.

Halfway through the concentration of tents, he tripped on a pile of firewood and fell on his side. He grunted and pressed his hands on the ground to get up. As he turned around, he saw something creep forward in the dim, yellow light.

It was tall and barrel-chested. On its wide face it wore a mask that donned two glass eyes and a jutting, rounded snout. Its uniform and helmet were blemished with dark soot and cloudy ash. Its boxy helmet was rusted and scratched.

Thomas watched in horror, unable to move. The sight of the mask burnt into his brain, reaching deep within and pulling out nightmarish visions. Within seconds, he recalled the fires and the blitz wardens and the piercing chorus of screams and wails. When he inhaled and exhaled and inhaled again, he could almost taste the blazing embers and boiling blood from the night the dragons came. He halted and stared. His pale skin shivered and crawled with bone-chilling memory. As it grew cold, it felt the relentless tugs and grasps and scratches from the crowd of masked Londoners deep in the dark underground back home.

Before he knew it, his hands were rendered useless. His finger vibrated on the gun's trigger but could not pull it forward. With widened eyes, he stood, all frozen and taut and panting for air. It was as if his senses had collapsed all at once.

The masked creature turned to its side. It had a large, slender, round tank strapped to its back. It reached behind and grabbed something that resembled a thick hosepipe. With its bony, gloved fingers it pulled the object to its full length, grasped a switch at the end of it, and with a *click*, the weapon roared.

Crimson flames shot right out the end. A thin pillar of fire drilled right towards the surrounding tents. With one long sweep, the creature controlled the flames in a swift arc. Countless hoards of supplies, ammunition, and rations were disintegrated in moments.

Thomas screamed and flung himself behind a rock. He covered his face as boiling-hot tears gushed from his aching eyes. After panting and sniffling and wiping the moisture from his cheeks and nose, he choked violently on the dust on the ground and the cramp in his throat. Though the muted gunshots around him grew crisper and louder, he felt tied down to the ground as if his bones were made of lead. He shook his head hard, ignoring any instincts that prompted him to get up and run.

He curled into a ball and dug his nails into his bare legs. The tender skin broke, causing warm blood to drip down into his shoes and socks. But to him, it mattered little; all he could feel and hear and taste and smell were fragments of what he had seen.

His breathing spiraled out of control. With clenched teeth, he waited for the creature to come and free him from his misery. But it never did.

What happened? he thought, tilting his head. He mustered enough courage to open one of his eyes and look above. The intruder pointed the hosepipe towards one of the larger tents. As the flames consumed the side and set it ablaze, two Rats jumped out of the front flap and started to holler. They scrambled around, patting down their clothes and extinguishing any small embers that caught on. With large eyes, they looked around for the source of the fires. To their confusion, however, they saw nothing, for the beast had now fled.

As the tents burned brighter, the fire spread even more; like a devious spirit, it jumped and bounced from one object to another. In time, the two Rats sounded their bugles. With great haste, the others woke up and rushed out of their beds. Like panicked schoolchildren, they backed away from the encampment and tried to gather water to extinguish it.

In time, the shooting had ceased. The fierce echoes of gunshots and yells faded away. With tense hearts and unsteady hands, the British lowered their weapons and stared at the dead bodies of the three trespassers. As the camp continued to burn, the men regrouped and huddled close.

Few were wounded. Some suffered from scrapes and abrasions from stumbling and dodging the Germans' attacks. Others had a deep burn or a grazed limb or a throbbing ankle. But the bloodiest among them was Lance Corporal Barkley. Still on the ground, he grasped his wet shoulder and winced in pain.

"I knew it. I knew it!" he growled, facing the Company. "Reinforcements...argh! Because of you, our medic and lieutenant are dead! Why, I'd wager that you clumsy fools started the fires as well!"

"Now, wait just a mo!" the pipe smoker griped. He stepped in front of his fellow infantrymen, stomped towards Barkley, and poked at his chest. "You can't just blame us! We tried to help you! None of us saw this coming."

"Oh?" Barkley spat. "And you all had one job. Yet, you failed! Mind you, if we Rats had just handled it, this fight would have ended much quicker and much cleaner!"

He held his wound tighter, pushing the pipe smoker away with his other hand. Pacing around in circles, he searched for any man who held the slightest sign of guilt. Before long, in the corner of his eye, he saw Thomas laying on his side and wiping tears from his eyes.

"You," the lance corporal growled, "you were the watchman of the southern quadrant!"

The Company gasped as Thomas whimpered and froze. In a split second, Barkley marched forward and withdrew a dagger with his right hand. With his left, he grabbed his shaking subordinate and held the blade to his neck. Thomas struggled a little and started to choke. Up close, his assailant reeked of alcohol.

"Perhaps I should let your little group know," the lance corporal snarled, "what happens to those who can't keep up with Mr. Covington's Rats!"

This whole time, the Company watched in fright. Eventually, they looked at one another with wide eyes and shaking hands, waiting for someone to make a move. Finally, the youngest Companyman bared his teeth and started to hyperventilate.

"Why, you...you let him go!" he yelled, voice break and all.

Quick as lightning, he and two others charged forward and tackled Barkley to the ground.

And with that, a fight had ensued. Both Rats and Company launched themselves at one another, yelling and pushing and barking away. The only one who stayed out of it was Thomas, who was crawling away from the group with his head down low.

Soon, they drew blood. Some shoved their foes to the ground while others jabbed their opponents with sharp stones. Thomas watched with gaping eyes as a few men had tumbled down the cliff. With pure rage, they staggered to their feet mid-roll and charged back up like raging bulls. Before they could withdraw their knives, the sound of a gunshot pierced the air. The men ceased their fighting and swiveled their heads. When they looked back, they saw Mr. Covington, standing in the middle of the fighting grounds and pointing his gun at the navy-blue sky.

"Who among ye started this scuffle?" he demanded. "Speak now, for I must know."

At this the men said nothing. They shifted their eyes to and fro, waiting for someone to speak up. Eventually, their gazes turned towards Thomas, who, still on the ground, tried to look away.

The poor man felt a chill zigzag down his spine. His heart dropped as he felt every pair of eyes stare him down. In the corner of his vision, he saw Mr. Covington stalk towards him with the gun still in his hand. In response, he started to pant and sniffle and wheeze uncontrollably. The sharp ache in his throat returned as a hot stream of tears ran down his face.

The staff sergeant stopped in front of him and tapped his foot. Thomas still averted his gaze. Closing his eyes, he waited and waited for ill words and ill treatment.

Mr. Covington said nothing. He holstered his weapon and withdrew his pipe. Sticking the thin end in his mouth, he reached into this other pocket and grasped a small, silver lighter. Popping the cap open, he triggered the sparkwheel and out burst a strong flame.

Thomas let out a cry as the yellow wisp dimmed a little and wobbled in the dark. He covered his face with one arm and used his other to crawl away. The crowd watched as he averted his eyes and continued to sob.

But Mr. Covington did not look angry at all. The expression on his face did not show malice or cruel intent; instead, his cheeks and brow were loose and relaxed. With slow grace, he leaned down and sat on his haunches. His long blue overcoat trailed close behind him like the robe of a king. He took a deep breath and exhaled. A slow puff of smoke escaped his cracked lips. After inhaling and puffing and inhaling again, he slid the pipe out of his mouth and held it in front of Thomas's face.

Thomas flinched as he saw the smoke dance in the wind. After hesitating for a moment, he gently bit the end of the pipe. Breathing in sharply through his mouth, he coughed out a dirty grey cloud. But after trying it again and again, he let out loose, steady puffs and soon ceased his grizzling.

"Now, lad," said Mr. Covington. "I know ye think that I mean ye harm, although that be not the case. Instead, I ask but one question."

He leaned a bit closer.

"Tell me. What did ye see?"

Thomas sniffled and wiped a tear from his cheek.

"I saw...I saw..." before he could choke up, he inhaled through the pipe once again. "I s-saw a man. He wore a mask."

"Did he spew fire?"

"Aye, sir. He spewed."

"Did he roar like a serpent?"

"Aye, sir. He roared."

"And what did ye do?"

"I hid, sir. I hid."

Mr. Covington nodded. He placed a hand over his mouth and remained deep in thought. Clenching his fist, he stood up and faced the throng of Rats and men.

"Well?" said he, "Ye heard him. Did anyone else see the beast? Anyone?"

The soldiers looked at each other with puzzled faces. They gave no answer.

"Very well." said the staff sergeant. "In all likelihood, he slunk back into the inferno from whence he came."

"Oh, and who's fault is that?" Barkley snapped, pushing away the others in front of him. His uniform was drenched in dark blood. He pointed at Thomas with a shaky hand.

"I didn't hear him sound the horn. Not a single note. I doubt he fired his weapon or drew his blade. I'd say he was slacking on his duties. No wonder the enemy slipped past. Surely, he deserves punishment, sir!"

Most of the Rats shouted in agreement. They shook their fists and pointed with sneering faces. Thomas trembled and bit down harder on the pipe's end, leaving a dent.

Mr. Covington sighed. But before he could respond, someone had scrambled from behind the grand Cromwell.

It was the youngest of the Company. His clothes were punctured with bristles and blackened with soot. He huffed and wheezed as he wiped the sweat from his brow. With his arms, he cradled an object.

"Look and see!" he piped in between breaths. "I don't know how I found it, but I did!"

He dashed to Mr. Covington and handed it over. The staff sergeant grasped it slowly and inspected it well.

It was cone-like in shape and dark in colour. Its metal hide had red splotches of rust. Though it looked quite bulky and quite thick, it was somewhat lightweight. And on one end it had a small, silver pin.

"Where did ye find this?" Mr. Covington asked.

"Down by the tank," said the youngest. "When...someone shoved me."

The staff sergeant held the cone by the tip, letting it dangle below his hand. Pulling the pin with his teeth, he faced the Locker and threw the whole object in it. After a few seconds, a harsh explosion resonated from the bottom. A flash of light gleamed below and disappeared with a trail of thick smoke. Once it cleared, the staffie put on a grave expression and faced the crowd.

"Why that, my friends, be a bomb. Say 'aye' if ye understand."

Everyone, with the exception of Thomas, gave a mighty "Aye!" and straightened their backs.

"And so," said Mr. Covington, "I see they were trying to ambush us. Rid us of our vessels and watch us die. Well, humf! They can't get us that easily."

He straightened his helmet, turned to Thomas, and helped him to his feet.

"And what be your name, little one?" asked he.

"Private Thomas Atkins, sir."

"Well, Tommy," the staffie declared, "ye may keep the pipe and lighter."

He patted Thomas on the back and faced Lance Corporal Barkley.

"Slacker or not," Mr. Covington announced, "I'd say Private Tommy here has had enough ill treatment for today."

Barkley grumbled at this statement. To further his misery, one of the Rats whispered in his ear that he had lost his wager on whether or not Thomas would die. Cursing under his breath, the lance corporal withdrew a small bag of gold and violently handed it to the prizewinners behind him. Just as they were about to open it up and scoop up the loot, Barkley grabbed them by the shirt collars and punched their noses.

In the midst of the violence, the Company stood together, standing in front of their smallest and weakest members before turning towards their leader for help. Meanwhile, Mr. Covington continued to speak.

"Hush! My word is final," said he, "and regarding the ambush, I'm afraid we cannot stay here whilst the Locker burns. The Fox will know of our whereabouts if he doesn't already. If the serpent took a hasty retreat, why, he'd travel great lengths to tell his wretched master that Mr. Covington's Rats still live! And so, we must go."

"Go?" growled the pipe smoker, tapping his foot. "And where will we go? Hm? Hmmm?"

Mr. Covington chuckled. "Where will we go? Why, elsewhere! Far, far, far away from here. At least...before I finalise our direction on the map. We must- now, wait." He paused as his audience's eyes drifted away from him.

"Are...ye lads even paying attention?"

It turned out that the Rats and the Company were not paying attention. Their stiff gazes focused not on the staff sergeant, but what was behind him. Mr. Covington frowned and blinked and turned around mechanically. He pulled back his coat's lapels and grasped a cracked spyglass.

Out there, on the scarlet horizon, thundered a heavy blizzard of orange sand. Spanning nearly two-hundred metres in height and an unutterable length in width, it rose and expanded like a thick billow of smoke. It gave a loud, soft hiss as it traveled. And it was coming closer.

"Well blow me down," said the staffie, "I suppose we're leaving sooner than I thought."

He rolled up his sleeve and stepped towards the crowd.

"We have about a quarter to an hour to escape. If ye acquired an injury, then bind your wounds. If not, then store up your tent and gather your loot. Bury our dead and toss our enemy's sorry carcasses into the Locker below. I'll impart further instruction when ready."

The Rats shrugged and gave a firm salute. The Company, however, looked rather dumbfounded.

"That storm is headed right towards us," stammered the pipe smoker. "Can we evade it?"

"Can we evade it?" laughed Mr. Covington. "Why, we're Rats! We can outrun anything and anyone! Or, at least I think we can. Now make haste, whilst the air is clear and the winds are steady. Does anylad have any questions?"

A slew of desperate arms shot up.

"Ah, put yer hands down! I didn't tell ye to raise 'em!" the staff sergeant yelled. He laughed heartily and marched off, whistling an eerie tune and walking far into the darkness.

<u>Chapter 12: The Storm</u>

The men got to work in a split second. They rushed to their camp, plucking the tent pegs and tossing weapons to one another. With great speed, they quenched fires, folded clothes, and threw whatever was needed into their vehicles. As they lifted and heaved and packed and fetched, they belted out a strong, raging song that went something like this:

Behold! The Fritzes invaded our sea
Now let's use their blood to sweeten our tea!

Do sharpen your blade and take up a good stance
Oh, poor Mr. Hitler! He won't stand a chance!

So put on your helmet and kick at the sand
Shoulder your rifle and take back the land

Go into the desert and out among rocks
Surely a rat can outsmart a fox!

Thomas glanced back at the sandstorm more often than not. The larger the billows grew, the more nervous he felt. With chattering teeth, he swiped a tobacco tin and snuck behind Mr. Covington's grand tank for a quick smoke. He did it once, then twice, then again and again. And when he ran out of tobacco, he swiped two more tins and stuck them in his pocket.

After the camp was picked clean, the Rats and Company assembled. Mr. Covington stood atop a large granite stone and pointed at his grand armoured vehicle behind him.

"My crew and I will be riding in this one. We'll lead at the front and ye will follow. Now, ask me where you're going to ride. Go on. Ask."

This time, nobody said a word. After some awkward silence, a freckled Companyman rolled his eyes and spoke up.

"Whe-"

"Where?" said the staffie with a grin. "Why, in these of course! Do show them, Trev."

He pointed to the bulkiest of the Rats, who stood to the group's left. Next to him were three car-shaped objects each hidden under a dark dust cover. Though they were sturdy and quite box-like, they weren't very large or grand; in fact, they each looked only slightly taller than a grown man. With meaty hands, Trev pulled off the tarps and laid them aside.

The Companymen gasped in awe. The mysterious objects turned out to be smaller armoured vehicles each with a green coating and a rather stubby gun at the front. Their armoured hides had faded black drawings of rats and knives and other fun, horrible things. The group muttered to one another, pointing at the vehicles.

"That's it?" the pipe smoker grumbled. "Four tiny vehicles? Four?"

Mr. Covington scoffed and put his hands on his hips.

"Yes, this is it! What were ye expecting? Good quality?" he shouted. "Now listen. Everyone calls these 'light tanks' with those fancy numbers and letters," said he, "but I like to call 'em 'Sloops' because that's more fun. Now, ye probably learnt how to use these in your training or whatever, but unfortunately, I doubt that was enough. No amount of mock-up roads or mock-up sands can compare to that of the real North African front, me lads...especially if the front itself is trying t' swallow ye up!"

He pointed back to the impending sandstorm, which had risen high enough to cover the blue sky behind it.

"So, to fix this," Mr. Covington said with a hurried pace, "ye will be riding alongside two Rats. One will command, the other will steer. Your job is to man the guns and watch. I'm afraid only three of ye Companymen will be riding for now, since we have three Sloops and three Sloops only, but once we reach safer grounds, we can rotate or something. Since, as ye know, safety is my main concern!"

At this, the Companymen looked at one another with great worry.

"Rats, choose your men. The rest will ride in the spare vehicle to protect our belongings. Luckily, I know these lands and where to find shelter. The storm comes upon us, lads. Anchors aweigh!"

Once Mr. Covington left, the Rats convened and cast lots on who they would bring. Out of the fourteen Companymen who were left, the odds were in favor of the shortest and the freckled; with mixed emotions, the two were led away to the vehicles while the others watched.

Lance Corporal Barkley had the last roll. He now had a lengthy white bandage draped across his shoulder. Though his tan uniform was swapped with a cleaner pair, some of the blood still seeped through. Biting his lip, he threw his dice in his steel helmet. With his hands behind his back, he examined the numbers.

"Well," he said, turning around slowly. "the odds are in favor of Mr. Thomas Atkins. Where be you?"

Thomas gulped and stepped forward. He hung down his head awkwardly and looked at the Rats with nervous eyes.

"Well, then," Barkley muttered, "perhaps fate wants us to settle our differences. Tonight, you'll ride with Trev and I, hm?"

"I don't wish to fight." Thomas muttered. "Please, I don't. I don't wish to fight…"

Barkley picked up his helmet and placed it on his head. Kicking the sand lightly, he scratched the back of his neck.

"Well," he sighed, "I can assure you that the first trip will be short. Once we get out of here, someone else will take your place and you won't be stuck in a vehicle with me, hm? I'll smell your stench and you'll smell mine."

Thomas opened his mouth to protest, but Barkley grabbed his hand and shook it firmly. The two walked together as the rest of the Rats and Company went off. Thomas sighed and stared upon the ground with frightened eyes. With his bugle clipped to his hip and his gun wrapped in cloth and slung across his back, he followed his new companions to the third vehicle.

The Sloop was ready. With a large bottle of rum under his arm, the lance corporal jumped in first and hoisted the others up. With Trev at the steering, Barkley at the hatch, and Thomas manning the guns, the three took the rear and followed the others around the Locker's edge.

Chapter 13: Harsh Sands

The group traveled at marvelous speeds. As it glided along the shining sand, the red storm followed behind in the distance. Barkley pushed open the top hatch and squinted back at the site of their old encampment. Dirty clouds of debris rushed over it with aggressive speed. Like a ravenous phantom, the squall consumed the rising smoke and dying fires behind.

Even with the lights on at the front, there was little to be seen. Each dune or rock they flew by looked nigh identical to the last. With Mr. Covington's great Cromwell leading at the front and Barkley's small Sloop at the very end, the group traveled swiftly and silently in the dark.

Meanwhile, Thomas did not say a word. Hunched over behind the trigger of a large gun, he kept his hands still and shifted his eyes left and right. As the sand scratched at the vehicle's armour, horrible, ghastly noises echoed into the Sloops's walls. They shrilled and hissed, as if a wraith or a beast had raked its claws across the cold metal. Thomas closed his eyes shut. He let go of the weapon and covered his ears with his frigid hands.

The rumbling and screeching and whistling grew louder and louder. For a brief second, the sight and sound of the Firebreather struck his head. Trembling, he reached for his pipe and lighter. Before he could slide his hand into the pocket, he froze and clenched his fist. He dared not smoke in the vehicle. It did not seem right. Sighing, he put his hand back on the trigger and tried to divert his attention towards other things. After looking down at his shoes and up at the ceiling, he glanced at Barkley, whose bristly umber hair flew back in the wind.

Thomas longed for the cool air. He took a fresh inhale to try and breathe in what he could, but he was still too far from it. Hoping that the air would reach him instead, he stared up at the hatch and watched the luminous stars dance in the sky.

"I know that look." mused Barkley. "You want to take a peep outside, hm?"

Thomas turned red at the comment. He looked away and flinched.

"Well, I!" he quaked. "You, you, I didn't-"

"Oh, don't deny it," said the lance corporal. "Here, just climb over already. I'll show you briefly."

Thomas gave a relieved exhale and clambered over. He popped up next to Barkley, squinting and smiling as the crisp air blew in his face. His hair flapped up and down as the vehicle accelerated. Looking to and fro, he watched the dark dunes speed right by. As the sand and cool air tickled his hair, he laughed like a child and placed his hand flat above his eyes.

While Thomas enjoyed the fresh air, he also grew tired of the silence. He cleared his throat and turned to Barkley.

"H-how fast can we go?" he chuckled, leaning over and looking down at the rough terrain.

"Oh, quite fast." Barkley said as-a-matter-of-fact-ly. "That storm wouldn't catch up if it tried."

Thomas gasped a little. He had forgotten about the storm. Turning around, he looked at the massive squall ahead and squeaked.

The red cloud loomed over them only a hundred metres behind them. It crawled forward, thundering and gnawing and scratching away. It swept over and under everything in its path; even the twinkling stars above were consumed by the rolling dust.

Thomas turned around again and narrowed his eyes. In the dim shine of the headlights, the rest of the vehicles resembled small, fading silhouettes.

"Couldn't catch us? Couldn't catch us?" Thomas exclaimed. "Look at the others! We're so far behind! Why, we should tell Trev to speed it up."

But Barkley shook his head.

"Nay, that won't be necessary." said he. "The storm cannot catch up to our vessel. But it can sure catch up to you!"

Before Thomas could even think about what that meant, Barkley struck him in the face.

Thomas staggered back from the blow, hitting the edge of the hatch. For a second, he saw stars. He grunted loudly and shook his head as the lance corporal grabbed his unbalanced legs and heaved them upward.

"Hey, hey!" he shouted, shaking tremendously.

He gripped the rail and tried his best to kick back. But no matter how much he fought, it was no contest; with a grin, Barkley heaved one last time and pushed his victim over the edge.

Poor Thomas let out a cry as he flew a metre back. He tumbled round and round in the air until he landed in the soft sands below. The loose grains scattered and hissed as he bounced and rolled over and over. Landing flat on his stomach, he groaned in pain and narrowed his eyes.

In the distance, the Sloop rolled away. Barkley still stuck out of the hatch, snickering and grinning and whooping like a hyena.

"Farewell and adieu, brave one!" he sneered, removing his helmet and waving it in the air.

"Tell the sour ol' Devil that it was I who damned you to Hell!"

In response, Thomas curled back his lip and reached for his gun. But before he could make a move, Barkley ducked his head and shut the hatch. As his vehicle climbed up and over a hill, the last of the dim lights had faded.

All was dark. The screeching winds whirled from behind. Thomas pressed his hands on the ground and pushed himself upward. Wobbling, he stuck his arms out and tried to keep his balance. A large, turbulent screech was let loose. It grew louder and louder. Shaking, Thomas slowly turned his head around and stared with frightened eyes.

The sandstorm had crept above him. It hissed like a beast and charged forward. With naught but the light of the stars to guide him, the poor man whimpered and picked himself up. He sprinted for a short distance, tripping over his own feet and staggering up again. He ran and he ran and he ran some more, refusing to look back. But no matter how hard and how fast he went, he couldn't escape; with a thundering screech, the storm lunged forward and swallowed him up.

He screamed as he was engulfed by the squall. Sharp crystals of sand scratched and clawed at his face, blinding him and seeping into his ears and clothes. The bellowing wind howled and cackled as if it were mocking his misery.

"Help! Somebody, please!" he yelled, struggling to keep his balance. Nobody answered. As he inhaled, small grains and shards blew into his mouth. Suffocating greatly, he buried his nose into his shirt.

Thomas wheezed and sputtered. He tried opening his eyes but saw nothing, for the last light of the stars had been snuffed out. The gun on his back and the items at his belt felt thrice as heavy. He covered his face with his helmet, stuck his hands out in front of him, and marched forward.

Blindly he trekked. He coughed and screeched and grunted until his throat bled. And when he had exhausted all his strength, he collapsed. Down a steep dune he rolled, limp as a ragdoll and weak as a worm. With a faded *thud*, he landed one last time. He sunk deep into the sand, twitched a little, and ceased all swift movement. On his side he remained, with his back turned against the deafening storm.

<u>Chapter 14: Harsher Lands</u>

The sun was awake. The beast was now tame. The birds who once fled from its wrath had returned, fluttering in circles and chirping with glee. Though the stars had hid when the light crept in, the thin wispy clouds up above took their place. The rolling dunes, now much taller than before, glistened hotly in the golden sun.

But poor Thomas still hadn't moved. Overnight, the gale had flipped him onto his back and buried him under a thin layer of sand. To the naked eye, he was nigh invisible. But he was there. And he was alive.

He woke with a sputter and a weakened cough. His helmet still covered his face. As soon as he gained consciousness and blinked thrice, he stuck his arms out and sat upright. For a good minute, he remained still.

A wave of blood rushed to his head. He winced as his limbs ached and his bones throbbed. His scalp felt like it was sizzling. He inhaled sharply to take a breath, but some loose sand had caught in his throat. Wheezing violently, he yanked the helmet off of his face and hacked into his sleeve.

The light was blinding. The desert was silent. Thomas grumbled before twisting around, getting on all fours, and clumsily pushing himself up. The sun's rays beat down on him hard as he hunched over like a withered plant. His forehead oozed with sweat, which rolled down in large drops and stung his eyes like salt from the briny.

Something hit his leg softly as he took a step forward. It made somewhat of a bubbling noise. Thomas looked down and gasped when he noticed that the canteen at his hip still swished with liquid. Without a second thought, he grabbed it and twisted the cap open.

He thrust his head back and took a long, clumsy swig. The water was boiling hot. Some of it trickled down his shirt and into his eyes, burning whatever dry skin it touched. But the poor man cared not; in a matter of seconds, he finished it all in one go and licked his lips clean. With a sigh, he closed the bottle and clipped it to his belt. His chapped, reddened face felt hardened and warm. Wincing quietly, he strapped his helmet onto his head and exhaled under its shade.

Wiping the sand off his arms, he looked down at his waist and started to count whatever other belongings he still had. He wheezed in relief as he grasped his knife and bugle. Gleaming with sizzling sunlight, they hung from his belt untouched. His gun, still protected by cloth, was strapped to his back.

Thomas looked ahead and behind. All he saw were rolling hills and open desert. There were no footprints or tank tracks or any sign of the Rats and the Company.

"No, no no!" he cried.

He paced around in circles and loops, grasping the top of his head and muttering to himself. Never before had he felt so lost, so small, and so alone. Round and round he went, trying to remember what had happened the day before. He remembered the Sloops and the sandstorm. He remembered the hatch and what it felt like to fall out of it. And then he remembered the name of the man who had banished him.

"Lance Corporal Barkley..." Thomas whispered as he kicked at the sand in rage.

"Lance Corporal Barkley! Ha! That crook. Because of him, I'll be dead by nightfall!"

He snorted and huffed. Looking up at the sky, he inhaled sharply and shook his clenched fist in the air. He tried to scream but a dry cough came out instead. Sniffling, he reached for more water but remembered that he had none. With great frustration, he decided that all he could do now was look for some more. Shriveling under the sun, he began to march.

Over and down the dunes he went, shuffling his feet and staring at the ground. He knew not where he was headed or where he would end up. But he knew how to walk, and that was enough.

The landscapes all looked the same. It was as if the entire planet was covered in an endless blanket of golden sand.

"Oh, sand...sand! Sand!" Thomas croaked, squinting into the horizon. He repeated the word over and over again until he was sick of it. Soon, he grew lost in thought, thinking about sand and its origins and wondering how there was so much of it in the world.

Faded memories seeped into his mind. In short bursts, he remembered the small piles of sand at the glass factory back home. Ever so slowly, he and his colleagues would pick up rusty spades and use them to cast those weighty piles into the dancing fires. Soon, with the right tools and the right temperatures, they were moulded and cooled and transformed into beautiful, beautiful glass. But now, things were different. Thomas never imagined the possibility of being drowned and lost in the very same material that once brought him purpose and joy. He frowned and laughed at the irony. It didn't seem fair.

Up above, the white sun scalded his bare arms and legs. Though the helmet protected his face, his dry brain felt taut and narrow, as if a tight band had constricted around it. He huffed and snarled and glared at the sky.

"Oh, God blimey!" said he. "How mighty is your wrath? First, you taunt me with too much darkness, and now, you curse me with too much light!"

Looking down, he grumbled and growled as deep, miserable thoughts swirled in his head and swam in circles like fish in a pond. His weak bones throbbed and cried under his skin while the dry air ate at his lungs. And yet, he trudged on, steaming and fuming and aching away.

At one point, he thought he found water. Up and ahead, between two rolling hills, he saw what looked like a blue, sparkling lake. He rubbed at his eyes and smiled with glee, mustering enough strength to sprint right over. With a cough and a wheeze, he scurried like a mouse. The calm waves ahead wobbled and shined brighter and brighter. He could almost taste the sweet, shimmering droplets. As soon as he came close enough, he sprung forward and held out his arms, ready to plunge into a cold pool of liquid glass.

But instead, he received a mouthful of sand. For the lake was not filled with water at all; in fact, it was never there in the first place.

Thomas felt like a fool. He screamed into the ground and beat at it with his fist. Once the sands grew too hot and bit at his bare skin, he had no choice but to get up and keep walking.

As he went forward, the colour of the sands started to change. Here, the bright yellows and tans looked more saturated and grey. And scattered around these newfound dunes were brown, jagged, misshapen rocks. They varied in size and shape; some were pointy and tall while others were stubby and stout. Like ugly, crooked buildings, they stuck out in the sand, basking in the heat and casting gnarled shadows upon the ground.

One rock in particular caught Thomas's eye. It was as tall, as long, and as wide as a man. And though it looked rather narrow. the very tippy-top of it broadened, resembling a thin, rounded helmet.

But Thomas did not know that it was a rock. His muddled brain and glassy eyes told him otherwise. With a desperate look on his face, he rushed forward and tried to call out to it.

"Hullo?" he hollered, jogging towards the object. "Oh, finally! Am I glad to see someone else out here. Pray tell me! Where's your encampment?"

As expected, he received no answer. For everyone knows that rocks cannot speak unless God wills them to. And poor Thomas, of course, knew this quite well. But under the dizzying sun and the steam from his skin, all he could see was another infantryman.

Thomas blinked. His smile faded.

"Hey," he whined, "are you listening? I'm speaking to you!"

Still no answer. Before long, the poor man lost his patience.

"Please," he cried, "don't leave me here! Come on, I know you know better!"

Soon, he began to shake it and curse at it and berate it. With aching feet, he kicked it so hard that his leather shoes tore at the soles. But no matter what he did or said, the rock gave no response. Eventually, Thomas wore himself out and gave up.

"Fine, have it your way!" he yelled. "If you wish to die out here, then be it so!"

Giving the object one last kick, he stormed off and continued his trek.

It did not take long for the hunger pangs to come. At first, he felt a small hole gnaw at the bottom of his stomach. But with every step and every breath, it only grew deeper and deeper. Thomas clenched his abdomen and whimpered. His vision was blurry. The small dune he had climbed now felt like a mountain. He coughed and groaned and stopped walking for a while. And when he had panted and fumed enough, he fell right on his back and into the sand.

The sun looked like it had risen much higher. With his helmet pushed back, poor Thomas felt his face sizzle in the sky's wrath. He wanted to cry but no tears ever came. With a long, drawn-out exhale, he started to close his eyes in defeat.

But then he saw a shadow up in the sky.

It was thin and quick. It had a long neck and two flapping wings. It moved with graceful speed, fluttering through and around the wispy clouds above.

Thomas flinched. He thought he was seeing a dragon. Before he could get ready to duck and hide, the creature flapped once, and a pale feather broke off of its wings. Down, down, down it swayed, tilting in the wind and floating around and around in great loops.

By now, Thomas had forgotten about the existence of birds and other creatures. This caught him by surprise. Shaking his head, he rubbed his eyes and blinked, waiting for the animal to fade into nothing. And yet it never did. In the blue sky it soared, circling once before gliding away in a straight line.

Thomas sat up and got on his feet. Without thinking, he started to stumble down the hill and chase the pale creature. He did not know how far he could run or if he could catch up. But no matter where the bird went, he followed.

He jumped and dashed in short bursts. His lungs felt punctured and swollen. His vision was dizzy and sore. He tried to grunt and yell and scream and cry, but his dry tongue stuck to the roof of his mouth.

Just as he was about to collapse once more, he looked ahead and stopped in his tracks. Out there, sticking out from the hilly horizon, was a rather tall jade tree. Further ahead, scattered around it, were clusters of short bushes and shrubs and other dense foliage. And best of all, running right between them and the sands, snaked a clear, crystalline river.

Chapter 15: River Agheila

At that moment, Thomas had forgotten all about the bird. Smiling hastily, he set his eyes on the oasis and picked up his pace. Though his chest felt like it was going to burst, he kept going. Once he had staggered past the rustling bushes, he pounced at the stream and thrust his whole head in its waters.

He sputtered in relief. A wave of frigid liquid flooded into his head and over his skin. The river was real after all. As he ingested the water in large, mighty gulps, he pulled his body closer and closer until he was completely submerged.

Even at the bottom of the river, he drank. Plunging deeper and deeper, he let the cold stream flow through his dirtied hair and into his ashen clothes. At first, he had nearly drowned himself. With an enormous grin, he swam around and around and shot up to the surface, laughing and crying and guzzling away.

Once he had his fill, he dragged himself back onto the shore and knelt down on the muddied sand. But even after he had quenched his great thirst, something was missing. He felt full and empty at once. Furrowing his brow, he pressed his fingers to his forehead and tried to think of what was wrong. And then, out of nowhere, his stomach made a deep rumbling sound.

He grasped at his middle and scoffed. With panicked eyes, he looked around for anything that looked or felt edible.

At first, he contemplated gathering some of the frail green palm leaves scattered around the river's edge. With shifty eyes, he counted them as they trailed along with the stream's winding shape. But just as he was about to get up, he saw a bird land in the water.

This time, he had a much better look at the creature. It had long, twiglike legs and a curved, hardy beak. Its thin head was supported by a sleek, slender neck. As it flapped its wings with glee, a few of its feathers broke off.

Its wet plumage was pink and its eyes were bright yellow. But strangest of all, despite having wobbly limbs and a rather plump body, it moved with slow, elegant grace; with steady motion, it looked down, shook its tail feathers, and dunked its head under the water to drink.

Thomas almost drooled at the sight. With wide eyes and shaking hands, he picked up his rifle from the ground and pointed it at the unsuspecting animal. He fired one shot, then two. Both missed, dispersing some feathers and causing the bird to flee. Thomas huffed and stepped into the water. With a cold, hard stare, he steadied his aim and fired one last time.

He heard a piercing squawk. The bullet had hit the bird's wing. With a pained cry, it spiraled down and crashed onto the sand, struggling to flap or run away. Thomas lowered his rifle and let out a startled gasp. He crossed the river and sprinted towards the dying animal. Before it could crawl away, he stomped right on its legs and thrust the bayonet into its chest.

The bird shrieked one last time and twitched for a while. After some quick, shallow breaths, it gave one last dying gasp and eased back onto the sand. Its pink and white feathers, now reddened with blood, trembled softly in the wind.

Thomas lunged forward and grabbed the bird by the head. He dragged it around and around, snatching pieces of dry wood and throwing them down in a convoluted pile. And once he had finished, he tied the poor animal to a spear-like stick and flung it right on top.

With fumbling hands, he reached into his pocket. He grasped the pipe lighter but it slipped out of his fingers and onto the ground. As he bent down to pick it up, a string of warm saliva drizzled over his lip. The pit in his stomach cried louder. He could almost taste the fresh meat.

Trembling slightly, he grabbed the lighter and flipped the lid open. Using his dirtied thumb, he pushed down on the sparkwheel.

It clicked as usual. But no flame came out of it.

He pushed it again and again. Still nothing. Biting his lip, he grabbed it with his other hand and pushed the wheel over and over until his fingers bled.

"No, no, no!" he yelled. He screamed at the lighter and shook it in his fist. Kicking the sand, he turned around and hurled the object into the river. With a faint splash, it sunk deep below, never to be seen again.

Meanwhile, Thomas whined and fell on his knees. Shaking his head, he glanced back at the flamingo and crawled towards it. Grasping the bird's thin neck, he withdrew his dagger and started to cut the feathers away.

His efforts were soon in vain. The animal's greasy blood mixed in with his, making the knife slip and slice right across four of his fingers. Thomas inhaled sharply and cursed under his breath as his hand stung. Enraged, he tossed the knife away, grabbed the flamingo by the beak, and lifted it in front of his face.

Growling gently, he thrust his head forward and sunk his teeth right into the bird's almond-shaped body. Walls of tough feathers caught in his mouth, but he turned around and spat them right out. And as soon as he dug past the matted layer of plumage, he clamped down on the animal's warm, rubbery skin and ripped it apart.

He chewed and crunched and swallowed and slurped until thick, oozing blood dripped down his chin. He bit through bone and marrow, shaking his head left and right to tear each piece of flesh in two. And when a tangled mess of innards and tubes slipped and plopped onto the ground with a *splat*, he picked it right up and guzzled it down.

The heavy air around him sizzled and reeked of wet, steamy carnage. Plump, hairy flies buzzed around the scene looking for a taste. The sands were muddied and soaked with dung and bile. But Thomas cared not. He gnawed and crunched and mangled and pulled until his face and clothes were stained with dark, crimson blood.

When he had finished, the bird resembled naught but a wet pile of feathers and bones. Thomas cast the mush aside and lay down on his back, staring at the hot sun above.

He waited a while to rest. Small insects swarmed and crawled on his face. The dizzying stench beat at his nose. Once he had enough, he got up, turned around, and headed for the river for a drink and a wash.

Sighing, he dipped his feet into the waters. His red reflection rippled below. But just as he was about to bend down and scoop the clear liquid into his hands, he heard a loud squawk.

Thomas searched around, scouting for whatever made the noise. His ears perked and twitched, listening intently for more. And when he looked to his left, he had found it.

In the middle of the river, where the current flowed strongest, sat two more flamingos. They floated like little boats, dipping their bills in the waters and shaking their tails.

Thomas glared at them. A strong, frenzied fire burned in his belly. Breathing heavily, he snarled and charged into the river. The birds shrieked as he came. Before they could fly away, he grabbed ahold of their thin legs and hastily dragged them to shore.

The first one he tore to shreds with his hands. Blinded by rage, he plucked its wings and ripped out its beak before hurling the body back into the waters. The second one wasn't so lucky; after pinning it to the ground, Thomas grabbed it by the head and drowned it in the river.

The corpses slid with the current. Their blood and innards oozed and dripped down below, leaving behind a dark cloud of red. Soon enough, the steamy stench of the bodies grew stronger.

Completely covered in drizzling, red filth, the crazed man paced back and forth near the waters. He rushed towards its edge and kicked at any stones and twigs in his way. When he finally grew tired and parched, he got on all fours and dunked his face in the river. And when he felt starved, he would pounce on an unsuspecting pink bird and quickly tear it to pieces.

Soon, the bugs and snakes and vultures and foxes snuck into the garden to pick the sands clean. But no matter where they scurried or flew, they dared not cross Thomas's path.

As the day trudged on, he spoke less and less. He struggled to conjure up any plans or ideas or cohesive thought. For hours on end, he laid waste to the garden, disturbing the soft sands and spreading blood on the ground.

In time, the orange horizon had darkened. The shadows of the tall, looming trees faded as the cool of the night swept in. Gathering his belongings and crawling under the bushes, Thomas laid back and looked up at the sky. As the crickets chirped and the river rushed, he eased into the soft sands and slept under the stars.

<u>Chapter 16: Fly the Colours</u>

Now, it came to pass that Thomas had circled the waters for several days. With each twist and turn of the river, he began to lose track of all time and place. Soon, he forgot all about the Campaign and the Rats and the lonely medic. He forgot all about Millie May and the blitz wardens and the deep, dark underground back home. And one by one, he started to forget all the good men and women he knew; the only familiar face was his own, which stared back at him when the sun beamed down at the river's edge.

His face peeled from the sun. His bloodied nails had sharpened and his hair grew past his ears. His necktie had withered away and his tan uniform was riddled with holes. But worst of all, no matter how many times he waded and bathed and swam and splashed, the dark, crimson stains on his clothes did not disappear.

One day, when he had run into the marshes, he made a discovery.

Sitting near the brown reeds, amongst the tall trees, was a shiny, metallic object. It had a bowl-like shape and a wide, flat rim. Thomas found it when the glare beamed at his eyes. He jumped and instinctively pointed his gun right at it. Backing up slowly, he covered his gaping, bloodstained mouth.

It was a helmet that looked much like his own, save for some extra rust and white scratches on top. Though its design was undeniably familiar, it had no strap or name or tag of any sort. After mustering enough courage, Thomas exhaled, shuffled forward, bent down, and lifted the object by the rim with both hands. Like a hot knife, a sharp, burning pain seared into his fingers.

He dropped the helmet and roared in anguish. He then looked to his hands, which had thin, red streaks from where the heat of the edges had cut.

He grumbled and hissed.

Once the object landed and sunk back into the sand, Thomas swung back his leg and kicked it as hard as he could. With a loud *pang*, it flew into the air, rotated twice, and splashed down into the crystal waters.

With his palms still open and his fingers still curled, Thomas rushed to the river and submerged his hands. Once the pain had subsided, he got up and searched for where the helmet had landed. But what he saw next made him flinch.

More helmets had littered the waters, spinning and sinking and washing up on the sands. Beside them floated other human possessions, including knapsacks, cloth, and worn, wooden boxes. Down the current they went, bobbing up and down like weighted buoys.

Thomas blinked. He galloped into the stream to get a closer look at the items. Just as he reached over to grab some of them, he heard a soft *bang*.

He recoiled at the sound. It came from upriver. With a raised brow, he stepped back onto the ground and looked ahead.

At first, he thought he saw evidence of a campfire. Indeed, a slender pillar of smoke billowed and rose from far behind the dunes, tainting the white clouds grey. Another *bang* ensued, creating more smoke and smog. A repetitive *pap pap pap* followed it.

Thomas huffed. He did not remember the last time he had seen or heard anything like this. Pacing back and forth and kicking at the dirt, he knew not what to do. Just as he was about to bolt down the other direction, he paused.

In the very back of his clouded, convoluted mind, he heard a voice. It told him to follow the trail of smog. He tried to ignore it and drown it out but struggled to do so. But in the end, he chose to listen. With reluctant eyes, he went on his way. Shaking his head and snorting sharply, he followed the worn, scattered array of helmets and clothes to investigate.

As he jogged along the water, more sounds filled the air. Some resembled distant screams while others sounded like swift gunshots. Once Thomas approached a hill where the noises grew loudest, he crawled on his belly and watched.

There, at the bottom of the dunes, was a scuffle. British troops, with their rifles and bombs, were being run down and fired upon from above. Dark bodies were scattered in the sands. Some were mangled and torn open whilst others were twisted and burnt.

As the air smelled strongly of blood, the smoke from nearby explosions rose higher and higher. Thomas squinted and ducked. He looked at the dune to his left and watched as a young German lay flatly behind it. In front of him, he had a cruel weapon. In loud bursts, it fired swiftly and accurately at the British down below.

Thomas looked down at his rifle. It had no ammunition. Snarling terribly, he glared at the German and withdrew his knife. With the blade in between his teeth, snuck up from behind and lunged right at the unsuspecting soldier. With brute force, he thrust his dagger into the man's neck and pushed it forward. As it pierced through, dark chunks of flesh and veins ripped out and landed onto the sands.

The youth made somewhat of a gagging noise and released his weapon. As he went to grab at his bleeding throat, he was seized by the head and cast to the side. Down the hill he rolled, tossing and turning before splashing into the river below.

Thomas grinned. He turned around and lay down, positioning himself behind the weapon's trigger. Gripping it tightly, he aimed towards the tops of the other hills and fired upon the Germans behind them.

They did not see it coming. Their faces and bodies were shredded and gored. Behind their similar cruel weapons they fell, resembling naught but red, boned ribbons and tubes.

But Thomas did not flinch from the blood. Instead, he glanced down at the slaughter below and searched for any surviving Englishmen. To his dismay, there were only two left; one lay on his back and choked loudly while the other screamed and gripped his torn leg.

Thomas bared his bloodied teeth and squinted, trying to figure out how to save them. But as he gathered his belongings, he saw a shadow creep near the dunes and sneak up on the wounded.

A masked figure had pounced on the battlefield. It held something in its gloved hands. Like a jungle predator, it traveled light on its feet without moving a single stone. The object in its grasp was long and slender, like a rope. It slithered around its bearer and fastened to a round tank on its back. And that's when Thomas remembered.

It was the Firebreather, still alive and well. Like before, he wore the same sleek uniform and carried naught but his flame-spitting weapon. His steel mask and helmet glistened in the ember sky. With his shiny, coal-stained boots, he hopped to the centre of the slaughter and looked around with glassy eyes.

But Thomas was not afraid of the Firebreather. He did not run or hide or call for help. Instead, with gnashing teeth, he placed his hands at the gun and aimed at his enemy below. With one eye closed, he pulled the trigger.

Nothing happened. It made a *click click click* noise but did not open fire. Thomas scoffed, fiddling with the gun and searching frantically for more ammunition.

For a moment, the two made direct eye contact. They stared at one another blankly, without making a sound. After a short, tense moment, the Firebreather shifted his gaze toward the wounded men on the ground.

They screamed and tried their best to crawl away. Before Thomas could get up and come to their aid, the Firebreather pointed his weapon at them and flipped the switch.

Scarlet flames shot right out. They engulfed everything, both the living and the dead, in their path. The cries of the two men had drowned in their wake. With one slow sweep, the Firebreather guided the fires. They engulfed guns and weapons and sands and soot, tainting the air with a dark, horrible smell.

By now, Thomas had given up on finding more bullets. He grunted, tossed the gun aside, and stood up. With a roar, he charged down the hill. Gripping his rifle, he leapt over the burning bodies and pointed the bayonet forward.

The Firebreather blocked the attack. Letting go of the nozzle, he grabbed Thomas's weapon and tried to yank it out of his grip. Consequently, the angry Englishman only screamed louder and held on all the more. After being dragged and tossed left and right, he let go of the gun and tackled his enemy head-on.

The two fought even harder. In the heat of the sun they wrestled, clawing and shoving and pounding away. The slithering hose coiled around their legs as they fell to the ground. Thomas bared his teeth and growled terribly, using all his energy to pin down his foe's limbs. Grabbing the Firebreather at the neck, he withdrew his rusted, bloodied knife and held it over his head. But before he could thrust it down, the masked German seized his wrist and squeezed it with great force.

Thomas cried out in pain. Thinking fast, he jerked back his other hand and grabbed the shaking hosepipe below. With a snort, he kicked the Beast in the groin, causing him to release his grip and fall back. With both hands on the serpentine object, Thomas stood over his enemy. As the smoke filled his lungs, he flipped the switch on the deadly weapon and roared as loud as he could.

Bright, golden flames spiralled forward. They shot out towards the Firebreather's face, burning loudly with strong yellows and reds.

The gas mask melted like butter. The Beast let out a ghastly, muddled scream. He kicked and shook and writhed upon the sands as his helmet and flesh were reduced to black, molten ooze.

Thomas yelled louder and louder. His eyes stung with raw, charcoal-tainted tears. Though his foe was now gone, he still held the hose firmly in front of him until the fire ceased to spew out of it. Exhausted, he let go and fell right on his side.

The sand around him had melted into black, sharpened glass. Thomas hacked and wheezed, trying to stop his poor hands from shaking. Nearly blinded by the smog and ash, he mustered enough strength to wheel his body around and look well upon what he had done.

From this angle, he could not see the Beast's head. All he saw was his torso and barreled chest, covered in burning, withered clothes and facing the sky. The smell was overwhelming and the sight was horrific. And still, he could not look away.

Letting go of the weapon, he saw something glisten from the dead man's neck. It was glassy and small and in the shape of a cross. Its corners were sharp and immaculate. Though its colour was obsidian-black, its shiny surface reflected the orange light like a mirror. Unlike the glowing, red flesh around it, it hadn't burnt or melted at all; like a bright silver star, it shimmered and shined in the dark.

Thomas coughed and squinted. He swore he had seen this symbol before. After blinking twice and leaning forward, he knew. Indeed, back in London, he had seen it; on the great, metal wings of the dragons above, the same black crosses glistered and soared in the charcoal skies. Enraged, Thomas huffed and puffed and thrust his right arm forward. With a bloodied sleeve, he reached for the Iron Cross and clamped his fingers around it.

A searing tongue of fire drilled into his hand. Like a hot mould, it sank deep into the flesh of his palm and stamped a burning shape in the middle of it.

Thomas howled in agony. He released his fingers and held onto his wrist as the metal badge slid down and plummeted into the sands.

He coughed and bit down hard. His hand vibrated and pulsed as the hot wound crept deep into his skin. With a throbbing arm and dizzied head, he looked around with great pain and sorrow.

He struggled to breathe. With his left hand, he took off his helmet, scooped the Iron Cross from the ground, and crawled up the hill. Of course, he only had enough strength to reach the middle of it; with frightened eyes, he scoured his surroundings for bandages, pills, or anything of the sort.

But what he found next gave him a different idea.

The dead Englishman closest to him seemed to lay on a crumpled piece of fabric. It was slightly torn and slightly charred, but still in one piece. Its pattern, which had faded with time and place, still donned the proud colours of the Union Jack.

Thomas grabbed the flag. With great difficulty, he tied it to his gun and stuck it in the sand. The light fabric caught some of the flames from the surrounding bodies, burning frantically like a flickering beacon. In the warm, ashen wind it fluttered, signalling a small yet strong British victory.

<u>Chapter 17: Cutlass and Cannon</u>

The sun was beginning to set. Under its light, the flag did not wither and the flames still burnt bright. Thomas leaned back and stared at the sky. Pressing his lips to the bugle and releasing a faint, somber note, he waited and waited, hoping for something or someone to come to his aid.

But what came next made him shiver.

At first, he heard a deep, rumbling, mechanical sound. He cocked his head up and down and all around, wondering if his ears were deceiving him. Just as he was about to lean forward and get a better look, something large had crawled up the hill ahead.

It had tough, metal skin and a strong, protruding gun. With its tracks, it pushed the sands away with great ease. And on its side, it donned the bold, black symbol of the Iron Cross.

Thomas flinched. Something emerged from the top of the vehicle. With a *click*, out popped a man who looked much like a commander. With gloved hands, he withdrew a pair of binoculars and looked through them with steel, cold eyes. As his gaze slowly turned towards the burning flag, he fixated on it and slowly lowered the instrument in his hands. But before he could utter a word, there was a deafening *boom*.

Something had shot at the vehicle. Indeed, a large metal shell had burst towards the hill. At a sharp, deadly angle, it bounced off the tank's front plate and struck the commander in a sight too gruesome for words.

Thomas closed his eyes a moment too late. He heard a crisp *clank* and a horrible *splat*. The tank was now smeared red with pure carnage. The remaining voices inside shrieked and hollered terribly at the sight. There was some rattling and some shouting and some brisk, angry words. Before the men inside could do anything more, their vehicle was struck by something else.

With a *thud*, a small object hit the tank's side and rolled onto the ground. The strange device left a pale trail behind it. Before long, the area was obscured by a dense, white fog.

Thomas swiveled around and tried to crawl up the hill. He wanted to know more about these attacks and where they were coming from. As he made his way to the top, he looked behind and marveled at what he saw.

Rushing along the river, amongst the bushes and helmets and debris, rode three small familiar vehicles. One of them had its hatch popped right open; sticking out of it were the pipe smoker and the youngest Companyman, shouting and waving and whooping foolishly as the other two sorry excuses for tanks trailed behind.

Right at the lead, with its grand cannon, charged the Cromwell. With terrifying speed, it headed straight for the hills as the Sloops around it fired another smoke grenade.

The German tank hastily fired back at the onslaught. Since its vision was obscured by the smog, it missed. Thomas watched as the projectile zoomed past the British and into the beyond. Laughing softly, he shook his head in astonishment as the pipe smoker and the youngest screamed in surprise and closed the hatch.

Shortly after, the Cromwell hooked around the hill and stopped right next to the German tank. In a split second, it fired one last shot; with a clamorous, chaotic, crashing noise, the second shell pierced the side and blew it to bits.

There were no screams or cries or calls for help; with the large gash in its hide, the steel beast broke apart and lay still, never to fire again. Meanwhile, the British vehicles parked around the battlefront, surrounding the masses of bodies and metal. Once the smoke had cleared, their hatches popped open.

Out of the Sloops jumped some Companymen, cheering and murmuring and galloping towards the fallen tank with great curiosity. From behind them came a few of the Rats, who pushed and shoved through the crowd to get a good look at the destruction.

After a good minute or two, the Cromwell's hatch opened as well. The first to climb out was Mr. Covington, blue coat and all. Twirling his pistol around his finger, he pounced onto the sands and put his hand on his hip.

"Well, me lads," he exclaimed, facing the cluster of dead bodies below, "I suppose ye did a mighty fine job."

"You loon." chuckled the pipe smoker. "Are you talking to the living or the dead?"

"Ha! Why, both!" answered the staffie. "Aye, both fought well. To the death and to the bone."

He marched towards the gutted tank and took a quick look inside. After a brief moment, he returned.

"'Tis a scuttle! And the crew is all dead. The captain himself is, er, half massed. So fly the colours as such."

Before long, the spare lorry pulled up next to the Cromwell. Out of it came the rest of the platoon and the section, carrying rations and drinks and other good things.

Thomas watched as the group planted their flag and cheered once more. In the midst of their victory, they still hadn't noticed him. Holding his torn hand by the wrist, he limped to the hill and collapsed on the ground.

The men all ceased what they were doing. Some jumped up while others stood back.

"Ho, Soldier!" said Mr. Covington. "Might I know ye?"

"W-what?" Thomas croaked, shaking the sand off of his face. "It's me! Tommy Atkins? Don't you recall?"

"Huh?" the staffie replied. "This can't be so. Tommy Atkins was just a young lad. What stands before us is a mad, heinous beast! And besides, Tommy died but a few nights ago."

"D-died?"

"Aye." sighed Mr. Covington. "Jumped overboard, right off the Sloop, he did. He couldn't take it anymore and just leapt. Well, at least...that's what we were told when he went missing, hm?"

Thomas grumbled in astonishment. He got up and pushed through the crowd, searching for the man who had wronged him. Once he had found Barkley, who was standing somewhere in the back, he pinned him to the ground, withdrew his knife, and pressed it against the lance corporal's neck until he bled.

"'Twas you!" Thomas bellowed. "You were the one who cast me out into the wilderness!"

Barkley stuttered. He knew not what to say. The Rats and the Company watched as he stared at his assailant with widened eyes. Of course, this was enough for Mr. Covington to notice that something was wrong.

"Lance Corporal Barkley?" he enquired. "Is this true?"

The crowd had gathered around the private and his prey. Thomas looked as though he was ready to slay the lance corporal at any moment.

"Fine! Fine!" Barkley screamed. "I threw him from our vessel, I did, but look at what came of it!"

He began to struggle, but gave up when he realised his attempts to break the beast's grip were in vain.

"Do you remember what he has done?" the lance corporal exclaimed. "When he stood there and watched? How we all could have been burnt up in our sleep? Oh, and not to mention the serpent is probably alive and well, roaming around these lands and scalding countless Rats and troops and innocent people!"

Of course, Mr. Covington had decided that enough was enough. With great haste, he locked his arms with Thomas's in an attempt to pull him away from Barkley. Thomas struggled to maintain his grip like a predator latched onto a small animal. But between the lance corporal's pushing and the staffie's pull, his iron hold broke and sent both him and Mr. Covington tumbling onto the ground.

The crowd hollered in shock. Before anyone could say a word, Thomas stood and shook the dust off his clothes. With his good hand, he scooped up the Iron Cross from his helmet and held it up for all to see.

The badge flashed in the light. Entranced, the men gasped and whispered amongst themselves. Even Mr. Covington, who was still regaining his balance, stopped whilst on his knees to admire the trophy of victory.

"The Firebreather is dead!" said Thomas. "He's down there in the pit with the others. Mr. Covington, you said that if we see a Nazi, we ought to bring him to justice. If we see a Serpent, we ought to bring it to Hell. And in less than a day, I did both. Now, the Fox is next. If I am permitted, I will bring him to you!"

He limped over and put the badge in the staffie's hand. With a scowl on his face, he stiffly tipped his helmet to Barkley.

The lance corporal glared right back and took a step forward. Before he could go any further, Mr. Covington marched in front of him.

"Well, I think I've heard quite enough." he growled, pointing his silver-blue gun at Barkley's face. "Lance Corporal Barkley, I'm afraid ye stepped over the line. You're hereby responsible for lyin', hornswagglin', and being downright terrible."

Barkley stammered for a moment before finding the proper words to defend himself.

"D-do you remember what sort of coward this boy was before?

Well, look at him now! He's...he's stronger for what I did to him that night, he is! R-right, boys?"

Barkley looked at the Rats and the Company, expecting support. But this only made Mr. Covington shake his head.

"Well," he mused, scratching his beard, "Aye, that be the case. But I'm afraid there be an upshot for this kind of behaviour. And so, Lance Corporal, I think it's high time for us to find out what your masterpiece thinks of ye!"

And with that, he walked over and handed his blue pistol to Thomas. The Company shuddered, taking a step back and huddling together as the Rats whispered amongst themselves.

Thomas looked at the pistol for a moment and thought hard. He gave a raspy sigh. After a few seconds, he slacked his arm, holding the gun near his side. Shaking his head, he looked down at his feet.

The lance corporal gave a desperate chuckle. He sighed in relief as his captor grabbed him by the shoulder reassuringly. But then, Thomas lifted the pistol once more and fired.

A slew of bright blood splattered upon the ground. Barkley dropped to the floor, clenching his gut. He looked at his hand, saw that it was stained red, and fell back. The crowd watched as he struggled a bit and tried to stand up only to fall again. He writhed and screeched on the ground for a while longer before slinking face-down in the hot desert sand.

The Company gasped, staring at Thomas with disbelief and disgust. Some covered their mouths whilst others turned away. The cold silence was broken, however, when a good half of the Rats cheered at the sight of such brutal justice. The other half, which included Trev and his closest companions, looked away with despondence.

Stepping over the body, Mr. Covington walked over to Thomas and wrapped his arm around his shoulder.

"Haha! Well done, me boy!" he boomed. With a large hand, he ruffled Thomas's hair and grinned.

"And so," the staff sergeant continued, "today has been a good day for dragon-slaying. I've made a decision. My fellow Rats and Company, give a cheer for Lance Corporal Atkins! Huzzah!"

At first, the entire Company backed away from the spectacle. Eventually, with some reluctance, a few of them joined the cheering Rats in celebration. Before long, those who showed approval of such a change bared their teeth and belted a song that went something like this:

Avast, ye sons of Adam!
Hold your bayonets up high
And tell fair Lady Libya that her spring will not run dry.

A thousand men have fallen
And a thousand will fall more
The day we meet that wretched beast upon that wretched shore.

A flash, a boom, a crack of the whip!
A glare of fire's light
Will make the dragon and the fox both cower at the sight.

And so, because of the charm of the jingle and the lust to burn the Fox to a crisp, the Rats and the Company turned to their leaders. Just as they hearkened and keened for new orders, they heard a sharp noise from above.

Up, up, up, in the bright orange skies, soared dozens of sleek aeroplanes. Luckily, their wings donned not Iron Crosses, but rounded targets. The British recognised the symbols in a heartbeat. They stared with awe and waved to their comrades in response.

Thomas looked up at the sky and then back at the Cromwell. Amid the gathering and the merrymaking, he did not feel as happy as he had hoped. With a somber look, he stared at the bloodstains on his uniform and the bloodstains on the German tank. As a good half of the men around him celebrated, he lowered his gaze to the body-ridden pit at the base of the hill. Though the cool breeze blew pleasantly upon his face, it still carried the soft, sickening smell of death.

"Death," Thomas whispered, squinting into the horizon. He repeated the word over and over again until he was sick of it. Soon, he grew lost in thought, thinking about death and its origins and wondering how there was so much of it in the world. As he grabbed his pipe, he looked down at the red burn wound on his hand and hollered for assistance.

Whilst the planes flew over the river, Mr. Covington noticed a slim, carrot-nosed figure walking over the dunes. He too had a round helmet and a dusted uniform. In his hand he held a medic bag and slung across his back was a gun. The hot, filthy winds blew at his red hair. Once the staff sergeant recognised the oncoming fellow, he galloped over and wrapped his arm around the man's shoulder.

"Dr. Callagher Huxley?" he called, bringing him to the others. "Well, this be a pleasant surprise! Where have ye been? How did ye even get here?"

At first, the medic said nothing. He watched as the Company began to remember the night he told them the tale of Saint George. With big eyes, they whispered to each other and looked quite relieved. Even Thomas, who was still lost in thought, stared at the medic with overwhelming bewilderment. He struggled to take this in all at once. Once Huxley looked back at him and saw his sloppily-bandaged, cross-shaped burn mark, he spoke up.

"Well, that matters not." he answered. "But some of your men are hurt. And that matters so."

"Aye, indeed!" said Mr. Covington. "Tommy, ye get over here first. Everyone else, I'd say you're in good hands. See, Mr. Huxley here is the best ol' sawbones that I've ever known. And if he cares to join us, then ye need not worry about split blood."

Thomas nodded and hobbled to the medic. Once his wound was bound, he did naught but sit on the tallest hill and watch the violet sky turn dark. Trailing behind, in between the blinking stars, flew one last British plane. It circled the sky, looped around once, and sped up to join the others. Thomas sighed as he smiled glumly.

"I suppose I am truly grateful and truly saddened," said he, "that we have dragons of our own."

<u>Epilogue</u>

When the British left the next morning, an eerie silence fell over the battlefield. The great German tank had cast a vast shadow under the moonlight. As a mighty wind passed over the river, someone emerged from the broken vehicle and stood on the hill.

It was the driver, who suffered few injuries but held his head high. For hours, the lad pretended to be dead and gone whilst the Rats and Company had their tea. Because he knew their language and practised their speech, he heard every song and every plan and knew every Englishman by voice and by name. Now that his foes had withdrawn from the scene, he gathered what he could find and went on his way.

For days, he traveled across hills and valleys and rivers and rocks. Through storms and gales he trekked, never losing sight of what had happened. When he reached his encampment, he demanded to speak to a very specific general.

In time, a meeting was arranged. The young lad was permitted to enter a heavily-guarded tent in a heavily-guarded city. At the seat, across a very long table with an intricate map, sat Mr. Rommel himself.

For hours they talked and convened. The driver told the Fox everything about the planes and the Sloops and Mr. Covington's Rats. He mentioned the river and the battle and the possible whereabouts of every single British armoured division in Libya. Not a detail was spared; each place and name and date and weapon was written in a file and put on a chart.

Once the Fox had learnt where the British were headed, he got up from his seat and straightened his hat. Promising the driver a reward, he left the room and watched the sun sink into the horizon. With a gloved hand, he rolled up his sleeve and crafted new, dangerous plans...

About the Author:

Janae Vasquez Seldura is a film and animation student from New Jersey, U.S.A. She is actively releasing pages for a noir webcomic called *The Graveyard Quartet and the Crowned Corvids*, as well as a plethora of other World War II-based stories. Her hobbies include traveling, reading, exercising, and playing the piano and ukelele. Though she does not have any pets, she has an aloe plant named Shredder. This is what he looks like:

112